Chapter 1

Back to the Trenches
✳ ✳ ✳

It had been an execution where the condemned man played a cello and his firing squad sang a song before shooting him. After killing the man we called Cello, they just turned right and marched off. How did they know he was dead? But it was not their job to care for him. They left the scene so untidy. The military tradition was spit and polish, everything neat and tidy and ready for inspection.

Cello's body was slumped forward. His abandoned instrument cast aside in the dust and grit of that little French farm square where we had momentarily held on to an impossible dream of redemption. The scene was just waiting for some little self-important corporal to come along and start bawling at the dead man to "Get this place tidied up! And what do you call this, eh?" pointing to the cello. It did offend military sensibilities, not being an instrument of war, but at the same time it was accepted unquestioningly by the firing squad. They had sung with gusto to accompany the playing.

I couldn't sing; my mouth was too dry. I just turned away, looking to die myself. Not in a tidy parade ground move, as so many deaths in battle were. There you could keep yourself in check and stiff as if on the parade ground when you went over. Here I couldn't have stood to attention for a second. Nor could I have marched. I could not have raised a rifle. I could not even see. My eyes were blinded by tears. Like a child, I stood there with my shoulders shaking. My heart hurt like hell, my eyes burned, and the tears streamed down. I couldn't stop them. All I could do was stumble away. I wanted to die, partly with shame for the crying, partly because of the sound of the music.

Afterwards I came to realise that I was crying not just for him but for everything about me in this war. I had to face it. I was a coward.

As his chosen "friend", I could watch his execution. He played his cello, and they all sang. I had hope then. The last two lines of the song he had asked us to sing—"I am the master of my fate: I am the captain of my soul"—were a kind of victory. But not for me. Afterwards, he just laid down his instrument and turned and faced them, no blindfold or anything. His face was calm, almost smiling. Then, without too much parade-ground fuss, they shot him, and I think every bullet hit him. They didn't rip him apart, which was strange, as those high-velocity rounds just passed through bodies into whatever was behind, in this case a wood-framed pit of sandbags. But some rounds would have tumbled upon hitting bone and could have taken away huge chunks of his body, as you saw regularly in the trenches. Yet these didn't. It was a dignified death, as if the bullets were being kind to the body they were passing through, just twitching the uniform as they entered with a little jump of dust. I didn't see the exit wounds. None hit his head.

In that final moment, his head twisted and he looked at me, standing to the side. He looked straight at me, and his eyes came out of his head towards me. Those eyes will never leave me.

After he got his cello, through the parcel delivery service, and I took it to him in its mysterious large box, which he leapt on in happiness; he knew what he was going to do. But the eyes still questioned me on the unsaid things. Those times we had together, before and during the court-martial, had been loaded with fear and a kind of twisted unspoken thing, which I suppose was loyalty to "comrades". Those same comrades that made sure he faced the court-martial. But when his eyes hit me, I knew with a kick in my stomach that all I needed to say was sorry. I hadn't said sorry. A simple thing, the only thing that was needed, but it didn't happen. Why not?

There were so many questions from the court-martial, so many deep things. I couldn't face them all, even fathom them yet. They pressed on me like voices, like the bombardment. I knew those voices would get louder.

I was weirdly free. As the accused's friend, I received no further call, and no one seemed interested in telling me to stand and fight, as they do

The
Cellist's
Friend

The
Cellist's
Friend

ROBERT J FANSHAWE

authorHOUSE®

AuthorHouse™ UK
1663 Liberty Drive
Bloomington, IN 47403 USA
www.authorhouse.co.uk
Phone: 0800.197.4150

Published by AuthorHouse   02/19/2018

ISBN: 978-1-5462-8833-6 (sc)
ISBN: 978-1-5462-8834-3 (hc)
ISBN: 978-1-5462-8832-9 (e)

Library of Congress Control Number: 2018901806

Print information available on the last page.

This book is printed on acid-free paper.

when you are in the trenches. Or when your comrades called, demanding your presence when you are out of the front line. You even have to join them at the toilet, the smell of each other intermingled so that we did not know it was foul. The swopping of lice to compare size, the cracking of them in blackened fingernails, the revealing of feet. Socks—the fouler they were, the more we laughed. Then we fought over clean ones. Our noses sniffed out the comforting smells of rum and rifle oil and the hot aromas from the cookhouse.

Anything was better than the smell of death, the overpowering putrescence of decaying bodies. It stuck inside the nostrils and down into the mouth, causing you to wretch. There was a horrific sight that went with the smell, of gleeful rats ripping the bodies apart. You had to fight the rats to get the bodies back for burial. You wanted to bury them for those two reasons, to get rid of the smell and deny them to the rats. The only good thing was that the rats reduced the amount of decaying flesh to bury. But they left the contents of the stomach so the smell was still ever present, and sometimes it exploded as you were trying to bury the body. After burial, the rats would burrow down to attack them some more. But so would worms as the flesh decayed.

What is flesh? What are bodies? Only when life is in them are they important.

Being free, I wanted to hide as well as to die. It should have been easy to die in the trenches; everybody else seemed to be doing it. That was what motivated me to get back there. That and the piece of paper in my pocket. It held the name and address of the person who had sent the cello. I assumed that was his mother. It was a strange box, the size of an ammo box but much lighter. Cello had said it was a "travelling cello", which folded down into the box. So the strings and handle and everything else were inside, including the bow.

I had moved from the Court-Martial Centre. I had a billet in a broken house with a straw pallet and even a broken chair beside it. It was a farm barn with many holes in the roof. People came and went. I had to go there and pack up my things and report back to my unit. I had to book out first and they would soon miss me if I didn't. Otherwise I could have wandered perhaps for days among these broken buildings and carts.

Hurrrrrrrrack Hurrrrrack. A truck with its croaky hoot made me move

3

off the mud track. It was full of laughing officers and their singing waved in my face. "We are not whining about the war. We are wining with the whores. Oh, bring on the women and the whores and we will not whine about the war." The sound whirled away as the truck rattled on. You never saw trucks on the front line. And women were just a rumour, and the rumour always talked of the officers' brothels or the staff officers going into the towns to drink with the women in bars and dance halls. No doubt this truck was one of those taking the staff officers into town for a night out.

Night out! It was not yet midday. I did not have much time left to wander blindly. I had to hand in my mattress and pack up my stuff, draw my rifle from the quartermaster's store and join the stream of soldiers heading for the front. There were streams always going each way. "What unit, soldier? Oh, they went up yesterday. Bad luck. No extra time off. Drop off first. Guides will meet you." Reinforcements joined units just as Cello and the others from the Artists rifles had joined us. Units that were incomplete or those seen as not fit to go into battle as an entity on their own often got used as reinforcements for other units. It was cruel to the new recruits. Just as you began to build camaraderie with those in your unit, you were split up and sent to join another.

You might go through the logistic area with its trucks and horses, as I did. It didn't seem organised, here in the rear area, but the army seemed to have a secret system for catching all its men and keeping them entrapped. A deserter would need to get miles and miles away before anyone caught him by the arm and questioned him. "What's your unit, soldier? What are you doing here?"

When you returned to your unit they hadn't forgotten about you. They ticked you off some imaginary never to be lost list and posted you back to your slimy pit of a hole in a trench, to be forgotten. When you were away you were important. When you were there, you were nothing.

I wandered about the logistic area trying not to catch the eye of an NCO. How could Cello have truly be said to have deserted while remaining in the front line? He had joined the German side—that's what did for him. Not to fight against us, never, but to collect casualties. It was sort of laughable but then so obvious. That's why it was laughable. He had been right all the time, right about the "mission" we had gone on, right to make a stand when Jack shot that other casualty. Was he also right to throw away his rifle? We went out to pick up a casualty but really had no intention of doing that. He was right that it was the screaming that had made us react. The screaming!

Now every shot would be like a scream for me. At every shot, I would see Cello's face looking at me. I had not shot him, but I had killed him. If only one other of us had joined him, one more had cast down his rifle in support, it would have been enough. But no, we turned on him to save ourselves.

I reached the pit, the sad spot that had been my bed. Surprisingly, or perhaps not so, the mattress was gone. The chair was still there with my kit. This had not been stolen. It was not mine though was it? What was mine? I don't know why it was, but then a sudden thought hit my stomach—possessions, his cello. I had the receipt in my pocket. Was it from his parents, his mother? But where was it? They would expect it back. They must have it back. I should be the one to give it back. I panicked and ran to find an NCO.

This place was controlled by the military police. I ran into one. "I … I have been on the court-martial and, errr, execution of Private Harris. He had a cello. He played it before he was …"

He looked back at my face, completely blank.

"It was his … he was sent it from home. I collected it and gave it to him before the court-martial … I …" I ran out of words, sweating.

He helped me with a cold, seemingly prepared speech. "All possessions of the, errr, deceased will be collected and returned to the next of kin, you may rest assured of that."

"Yes, right," I said, turning away. My heart and stomach settled a little.

The blackness returned when I collected my Lee Enfield.303. It came like a stranger, which a soldier's rifle should never be.

Shoot yourself, you selfish bastard. Do it now! A small voice in my head told me. I collected the clip of ammo we were allowed until we returned to our unit.

I had failed. How many failures can a man have before he gives up? But this was not the place to spill your blood. Who would notice? Who would know? "The deceased's possessions will be collected and returned to the next of kin." The fact that I had virtually no possessions, no cello or violin, no song of farewell, no special things, probably kept me alive. I was the only possession I had. I would return myself to my next of kin. Did I have one? Cello did, and I needed to go to her and tell her what happened. That was enough to make me try to stay alive.

I joined the throng, gave my unit name, started the tramp up to the line, up to death perhaps. Who would be there? Whoever was there would not be glad to see me—a straw pallet and the food cooked for you, night's sleep, nothing to clean. A soldier's needs are so simple yet never delivered. Except for you, lucky bastard. Nothing would be said of Cello. It would be a sort of guilty secret, like between naughty children. Would we ever speak of it?

It was a well-trodden mud road, great pools of water bridged by wooden structures, not bridges, just masses of wood stuck into the mud until it made a walkway. Dead horses, bloated and motionless, like large, smooth rocks, made islands in the mud. Then there were parts of country where the farmland was almost intact. But there were no farmers or any civilians. I had seen a few frightened groups in the logistic area, but nearer the front, none. We headed northeast, leaving the sun behind. It was a rare bright April day. Would the spring come in this wasteland? No trees to bud, only the broken stumps, lifeless. Some birds struggled on. But now the guns were heard more distinctly as we trudged towards the front.

We passed a few straggly bands of men coming back, but we tried not to look at them. For the first timers, it would have been terrifying to see these ghosts, some swathed in bandages, some being led with bandages around their eyes, uniforms in tatters, most carrying no weapons. Quartermasters would have taken them. Some formed groups marching listlessly back to rest. They carried their weapons at the shoulder. Respirator masks hung open on belts. I remembered the gas we had been caught in on that day with Cello. I looked sideways once and saw a man's boots flapping with one sole almost off the upper.

My feet! I looked down. Why had I not tried to get some better boots while in the logistic area? This marching made me aware of my feet. Good boots were like being rich, only available to the privileged few. Some guarded them shyly, and some flaunted them swaggeringly. When a rich man died, others gathered the boots. Before he died they would beg him to bequeath them. Double amputees were preferred to single ones. What a small and simple and brutal world being a soldier was.

Cello was different. He shone a light into this darkness and discovered the terrible things there and wanted to stand against them. No one stood with him.

We marched on noisily, a cloud of smoke above us. NCOs allowed smoking on the march near the front. I did not smoke. Some shouted and cried, "How long to go? God, we don't want to die!" Some bravado concealed the fear. "It's a long way to Tipperary, a long way to go." Others sang but not with enthusiasm.

"Spread out when we get nearer the front, open the distance. March easy," NCOs shouted.

I spoke to no one.

"Stop for water and a rest. Get off the road, everybody!" We sat down and eased our kit off our aching shoulders. I had filled my water bottle. I smoked then. There would be no food until we reached our units. I had some hard biscuits saved from the last meal. Those biscuits got everywhere. Often they were the last thing that men ate before going over. You saw the undigested bits gleaming white in their teeth as the mouths gaped open in their final gasps as they lay, cut down by enemy fire, some only a few feet from the trench they had just left.

We began to reach our destinations. Some of the anxiety had been replaced by laughter. Mostly there was silence. Paths led off to unit assembly areas, sometimes with signposts on stumps. Men moved off the track meekly, accepting anything. Shells began to crash rather than boom in the distance. The road would be a regular target. Some NCOs scanned the skies for aircraft that spotted for the guns. Sometimes our own guns replied. Wrecks of vehicles and more horses stuck out of the mud. We helped with a stuck truck, not full of officers. No personnel were allowed to travel by truck here. They only marched. Any officers singing and laughing, like the ones in the logistic area, would have attracted a hostile reaction and some words of disapproval from the NCOs. We had seen no officers on the march. Sometimes they rode horses, as though out for a morning ride while men struggled on in the sucking mud.

Then it was my turn to move off. For the first time I discovered that there were a group of us. I knew I could not be on my own any more. How many, ten of us? "Unit? What company?"

Gradually we got closer to the same little spot—the same trench, the same stench of nearby fresh excreta. It was always new and always nearby. Latrines were part of the trench system. Would the same men be there, less maybe some casualties? Who would they be? Would they be forward or back, battles fought and lost, or no battles? How many times had they been back to rest and back here again? Even if there had been battles, the activity would be no different—the night wiring patrols, the mending of the trenches and endless, endless sentry duty. The waiting for the next push over the top ... the waiting and waiting ... and the dying. Oh, for sleep until death.

Everything was heavy—the rifle, the equipment with its straps, rope stiff, pouches hanging from them with items crammed in, water bottle with its khaki cover, the water tasting of some chemical purifier, the uniform stiff, soon to be stiffer with the dried mud of the inside of the trench. The stomach twisted with anticipation and the heart felt heavy.

"Follow the guide, Alpha Company. This way."

We dwindled in numbers, then began to look at one another, but still no recognition, no speech. A tiny mud track, beaten earth around the puddles of mud, wire and unspeakable things. Boots followed in single file. You looked for possible jump-offs in case a five-nine shell came screeching over. None came. Then you began to worry about the quiet. Then, up ahead, voices on the evening air dispelled the worry somewhat. We joined the trench system, thankfully.

A slight rise in the ground, company headquarters. "Ah back from court martial duty, heh heh." Pipe in the mouth of the Sergeant Major, ticking off the list. The army was like a universe, your place in it like an ant, the dot point of a pencil on a grubby notebook.

Chapter 2

The Soldier's Loneliest Job
✳ ✳ ✳

Jack was there. He would never die. He was not pleased to see me. Bottle and fag in hand, he waved both. "Ah, Cello's friend. Shuffled off this mortal coil, has he? Gone to his maker? Silly fucker."

I looked at him hard, trying to show my disapproval. That would never work. The push and pull of power between men, ever present, stifled me, diluted everything I would say.

"So, what you looking at, son? Had a few days' rest and recuperation, have we? Good food, no doubt." Then he leant forward. "Get to visit the whore house, did you? Get your little tinker working?"

I put down my stuff. We were at the dugout, the same dugout. There was poison now between us. He knew that. He would use whatever power he had. Fighting your comrades, those who had been your friends before. That was only going to make this war worse. "Same spaces, is it?" I indicated the darkness of the dugout. Evening was drawing on, but I could see my former space was no longer a space. "Got a bit crowded of late, but don't worry. I'm sure we'll have someone leaving soon," Jack gloated.

I looked around at the other members of the section, their eyes dark holes, one on sentry looking through a trench periscope, a couple cleaning rifles, and one eating. I didn't recognise any of them. Nods followed. "Ben," I said. The nods ended. No one else spoke. The one man eating looked at Jack, waiting for the next shot in the power play. These were no Artists Rifles. They looked like returning casualties or those returning from extended leave.

Then the corporal came round a corner of the trench. "Ben, lazy fucker!"

I had no place here.

Everyone settled down for the evening. I was on sentry, obviously. Laughter came from the dugout. The sort of laughter when you know you are probably its subject. I had no idea who, if anybody, would relieve me. Perhaps I would spend the whole night here. The sentry, the most common of soldiers' jobs, some would say the easiest. But how to fathom an approaching attack or guard against it? How to wake your comrades when one threatens? How to stay awake (for sentry duty always came at the point of exhaustion, or virtual exhaustion)? I had marched some miles, yet last night I had slept a full if fitful night, uninterrupted by guns and rat noises at the edges of consciousness, if not in my face. I was the freshest of all here. Yet, as usual, the sentry duty hung on me as the lonely and solitary job it as. You were not alone with the enemy in earshot and the laughing, soon to be mothered by sleep, comrades near you.

It was at these times that I needed to think through the whole. Noises perked my ears. I had forgotten the detail of no man's land in front of us, and Jack of course had not bothered to re-tell me. A soldier had to remember. It was getting really dark, but early evening patrols would be out. A wiring party had passed through. They had sandbags to muffle sledge hammers. But there were some vague sounds … it could be. Wiring in the dark was almost impossible. The gloves were almost never available. Men used sandbags to wrap their hands. Looking over it in the morning from a periscope revealed some pitiful efforts. Why was it all necessary? The wire seemed no obstacle to a determined push towards our trenches.

The night progressed and deepened. The sentry becomes aware of the soil beneath his elbows, the rifle becoming colder in his grasp. Every distant or nearby light had a rainbow ring of eye-popping enlargement. That was when he had time to think. Otherwise the sentry was aware of nothing until a blinding flash of fire and the physical exertion of sightless hand-to-hand fighting came upon him. The smallest engagement—a sudden grappling with a surprise enemy patrol or a shell landing very close causing casualties—was like a pinprick on the battlefield. But to the sentry, it was like the whole war in one instant. You are very small and very large at the same time.

The small sounds were benign, I decided, for the moment.

My mind strayed. The song we had sang before they shot Cello. He had given me the words and I had burnt them into my brain. Then I wrote them out and passed them around to the firing squad. It was like a hymn sheet at the Sunday church service, compulsory attendance when not in the trenches. But somehow, as if by some miracle, the firing squad did not question and seemed to know what Cello wanted. They did not flinch either from the singing or from the cello playing or from the shooting. It was like a theatre. Was it therefore real, meaningful, or the nonsensical, the dumb obedience of an army?

The firing squad seemed controlled by Cello. He was their master and commander. Without orders or knowledge he held them, and they would have done his bidding, even though it was not his bidding to shoot him, but in a sense he had been complicit. The whole theatre was complete. He had drawn his bow across the strings in a mournful note, then started singing himself. The firing squad joined in. Then Cello upped the tempo of the music as he played with gusto.

"Out of the night that covers
Me,
Black as the pit from pole to
Pole,
I thank whatever gods may
Be
For my unconquerable soul."

The first verse. Yes it could be a hymn, that song. It was in fact a poem, cello had said, with music.

But now in the darkness and the loneliness with night covering me in this sentry duty, it was a statement: "I thank whatever gods may be for my unconquerable soul."

Even in this place, they couldn't take your soul. Not the court-martial, in Cello's case, or the leaders or the war or death.

But all that was for Cello. His soul was unconquered. He had stood up against us all and spoken and acted and then died, with his soul intact and therefore unconquered. Me, us, we had given away our souls, by murder, treachery, and then lies or concealment of the truth, which is just as bad.

So how was I to get mine back?

I knew this was what I had to do. I didn't know whether it would be possible.

Night was always a battle for sleep or against it as for a sentry. Early patrols were acceptable if you could get sleep afterwards before dawn "stand to". Late patrols interrupted the whole night. You always picked up a stint of sentry to interrupt sleep. We didn't have any patrols from our section on this night, but others passed through and back.

Shots rang out. There were always shots, maybe accidental, maybe suicidal, or a despairing patrol discovered, always lights, star shells going up, explosions and the strange ghosts of a dark warzone waiting for battle. Closer, an exasperated oath carried on the breeze.

It grew colder. Time was measured by an ancient watch carried by the sentry, the section time piece. Your relief had to wake himself, or you had to risk leaving your post to shake him, if you knew where he was sleeping. Normally you did, but I did not know whether I had one.

I wound the watch. A far-off flash enabled me to see that it was nearly midnight and suddenly there was a noise behind and below me in the trench. The long bayonet proceeding the rifle and the man. It turned and caught some ambient moonlight, like the spear of an approaching silent native warrior. The top of the helmet came visible. He looked up. "My turn now."

"Are you sure?" Stupid utterance by me.

"Course. I been doing the middle shift since I got here."

This was like a miracle for any section of soldiers, a man who actually volunteered for the midnight to 4 a.m. shift. But such men can be a danger. Why would anyone volunteer for this? What would be going through their mind, night after night, in the lonely vigil of the dead of night?

I climbed down the ladder from the sentry position. "Anything to report?" he asked.

"The patrol that went out through here is back. I don't know of any other that's out. All seems quiet," I said.

"Normal password?" he asked. Why did he ask that? They had told it to me.

"You know it," I said. Then, "What's your name. I'm Ben."

He passed up the steps and took his place as if it was his little castle. "They call me Midnight."

It seemed too good to be true. Too obvious, like a dependable young black horse. I looked into his face for the first time and discovered that he was a coloured man. He was as dark as midnight indeed. This gave me fresh hope of a friendship. "Where you from, Midnight?"

"Jamaica. They sent me across with the rum."

I smiled at him and liked him for his openness, although that joke would not last long with the rest of the section. Then I thought that with Jack's propensity for his rum ration, he might have come up with the "joke".

I stepped down and went to find somewhere, somewhere to sleep. Past the dugout from which loud snoring echoed, there was a slight indent in the wall of the trench. In the bottom of the trench, the soil was dry. A drain ran down the centre of the trench to the side with some broken bits of wood over it. There was a little water in it, or it was probably urine.

When the water came up to ankle level we tried to get some duckboards to keep our feet out of the water. When it came up to knee level we ripped up the duck boards to add height to our "beds". When it came to waist level we abandoned the bunker and stood leaning against the trench step like miserable scare crows with capes draped over shoulders, motionless, defeated, as the feet surrendered to trench-foot and rottenness and the body lost any sanctuary. Men slept there as they leaned, and if they fell, others had to drag them up or they drowned. Funny to drown with exhaustion, but some men just gave up, unable to stand and happy to go.

Now it was a dry trench floor and I sought some sanctuary, some innermost being, where my soul should be. I put my cape down and curled down on top. My small pack formed a pillow. My blanket covered me. It was almost comfort, if only because my feet were dry. They throbbed a bit from the marching, and that in a way was comfort, knowing that now they were resting, even though they were still booted. My helmet twisted over the side of my face as I laid it on the "pillow". My rifle was against my body, like a lover. But as to that, my hands sought to go inside my trousers, to pretend that they were some fair hands to hold and guide my manhood and bring it to a place of impossible ecstasy, which I had or had nearly experienced at some time in a seemingly different world.

My thoughts were of Cello and the things that I had to work out. But closer was this man who had relieved me, this Midnight. Somehow, despite their differences, I began to regard them together as one man. Both were open and generous. Both seemed to have a soul.

Chapter 3

The Joy of Digging a New Latrine
✳ ✳ ✳

It was April, and birds were doing what they do in spring. So even in that place of stenches and misery, I heard some starlings—I think they were starlings—singing before and as the dawn broke over the already broken gap in the earth above me. Then came the movement of men, the waking like a mist of melting metal, rising not with heat but as though from slime, the dredging up of life. Without a word, grey, grimy men climbed onto the step and waited to gingerly peer, with helmets like so many moon crescents, through the departing confusion of the night, towards a new, soulless day. There was no sign of the sun. But somewhere that bringer of light was there. Although why he bothered to break earth's sleep and not desert us to slow death, God only knew.

I took my place in the Stand Too, next to Midnight. This was the time for each side to test the nerve, of themselves and each other. Everyone knew that eyes were waiting in no man's land and in the other trenches. It was supposed that an attack might come at dawn. A newly placed Lewis machine gun could take a heavy toll if suddenly an unsuspecting Boche section showed themselves. Like us, they brought up new recruits, changed units in the trenches at night. So each morning, something new could happen. Uncontrolled movement could be spotted. Or if we showed ourselves a whole section could similarly be taken out by a Boche machine gun. This was the game we played, the careless, miserable game.

With a start, I remembered how one of Cello's colleagues had been hit in the neck and died right there in front of us. That was just in front of where we were now. We had dug shallow trenches to surprise the Boche when they attacked, then withdrew to these better ones after the Cello incident was all over.

Otherwise, it was the waiting and the ritual. Today we kept ourselves down, only the sentry taking down details through the periscope. A parade of people came along to check that we were awake. Sometimes a man would be told to strip his rifle. A sergeant would inspect it, then invariably start shouting at the man so that everybody else heard. How could you keep rifles parade ground clean in these ditches of slim and filth? A charge would follow.

Today, a lieutenant, whom I recognised as our new platoon commander, the sergeant major who had "greeted" me on my arrival the night before, and the colour sergeant, Q, who brought up the rations and the rum, came past us. They looked at our backs and went away.

"Stand down." We relaxed, then instinctively ducked down. A scream, not human, sudden, a thud, feet away. It seemed in front of the trench, an explosion and a heavy shower of mud and hot metal came into the trench. "Whizz bangs, perfectly timed. Get ready. They got lots of them, must have had an ammo re-sup," came a warning from the corporal. We crowded into the bunker. A few more came over, but no one seemed troubled much. Had they been new recruits, they would have started to shit themselves then and there. A fresh smell would have filled the bunker, and everyone would have looked for the telltale signs: the blustering blushing body language, turning away to find a toilet or just running from the bunker screaming, or even singing in mock hilarity—anything to conceal a pair of soiled pants. Often they were quite fresh pants and trousers as well for a new recruit, and it was sad that they should start by getting dirty like that.

But nothing was fresh and new for long, and the freshness came off the stench. Wiped trousers became filthy with trench slime, and the soiling was forgotten. Indignities were soon left behind in the trenches. What was important was staying alive, not keeping your shit in your body. It was not meant to be kept in there anyway, and the soldiers' language is mostly about it and the motion to produce it. It is only the way the words are spoken that signifies good and bad. The words are the same.

Eventually we left the bunker.

I sat down with my stuff and started rifle cleaning. Maybe some ration and ammo re-sup would come; otherwise, we would be told what to do. A soldier cannot predict or seek knowledge of the future, even the future of the next few seconds. All he can do is occupy the here and now, if it is not occupied for him. But he is expected to be ready for anything, have his rifle clean, be fed, and have a full water bottle, so spare time was occupied with these preparations—not knowing what for.

I had decided that I would keep myself to myself and take life moment by moment. Very carefully, I removed the now-crumpled piece of paper that held the name and address of the sender of Cello's instrument. This would have to be committed to unfailing memory, as I could not keep it in a readable state upon my person. I read it over and over, then tested myself on it while doing the rifle, having carefully put it in the chest pocket of my shirt, which was the one used only for fags and matches. Maybe later I would put it into a matchbox. I must learn it before it got thrown away, blown away, or lost.

This was my future. When contemplating death, we look into our future. I now had a future, which is very dangerous for a soldier. Fear came from the possible loss of that future. There could be the fear of physical injury or pain when you had to use the bayonet, or the trenching tool when face to face with the enemy. But in the moment of confrontation, adrenalin fuelled our response in a desperate lightning lunge for survival. Kill or be killed. But in the waiting and the occasional shell landing, there was little fear of physical injury. Shrapnel would tear you apart before you knew it was coming. If you heard the crack of small arms fire, it was going over your head or around you, not into you. Then the thump of the delivering rifle or machine gun could be heard a fraction of a second later. Yes, the whizz and screech of approaching shellfire made you leap for cover, and sometimes your flesh burned in anticipation of being hit, but that was a survival instinct. It did not necessarily create fear.

The alcohol-fuelled bravado lessened any fear. Or did it? The shared laughter in the face of shot and shell was more a ghastly grimace of false hope. It was always fragile and could be broken by a new face that brooked opposition, as Cello had done. Then the bravado turned to anger, directed against the one who was branded as weak. Fear made this happen. There was no courage in anger. There was no power to conquer fear in anger. I knew that now.

Courage was humble to accept the waiting with patience, to not put too much hope in the future, to not think beyond the here and now. And always to be unselfish, the opposite of bravado, which by nature was exclusive and selfish.

I could not extend myself to that. I could only look towards conquering the fear of loneliness. Bravado was one thing, a kind of false friendship. Cello had shown us a real friendship, which ironically was difficult to forge in the trenches. You had to start with a kind of illicit exchange, like a first liaison among schoolchildren in their pubescent years, desperately hidden from sneering classmates.

I exchanged glances with Midnight. He made a proposal. "You gonna work with me to clean out the bunker and sort out the shit house?"

A joy, to work with someone in the latrines, as the hierarchy referred to them. They were a source of so much bodily activity, conversation, and odour, the kind of centre of our world. So we set to with a will, united in effort and with a spark of shared ownership, just as the latrine is shared by all. The disinfectant stood in a bucket outside the hessianed-off hole, with its wooden hand rails and wooden seat, removal of which told you how close to the surface the human waste had become and whether it was time to abandon this particular venue and dig another. It was always close to the surface. Latrine fatigue parties were always looking to put off the digging of the next pit, which took effort and attracted blame for the new location, its depth, and its comfort.

Midnight did not shirk from the task of digging another. "This is totally full. We need to dig again," he said upon looking into the hole.

"I don't think there's many places left now," I said uselessly. Old latrine sites were normally doused up with detergent, filled in with soil and boarded up with any wood or corrugated iron sheets that could be found or acquired. Then you chalked a notice up. "LATRINE WAS HERE." Something more explicit and less reverent was usually used.

"We can use the other side," he said.

"Not towards the Boche."

"Why not?"

"Well someone might fall in," I said stupidly.

"The ladders can go over it."

"Sentry positions, and what about the fire step?"

"Okay. Let's look for another space then." Midnight seemed slightly bemused. I began to wonder about him. Was he really someone to entrust with your friendship, even in loneliness?

We found somewhere which was not too close to the bunker, but it was close to the other end of the trench where the junction was with the next section of men. A small mound separated the two trenches, and someone had burrowed underneath so that you could see and communicate with them and confirm the linkup.

Unfortunately, it rarely happened, and usually there was something of a disconnect with whoever was on the other side. They were not the same company. Officers and NCOs occasionally came along and spoke with men on the other side. Pieces of paper gave information of patrols going out and back. The sentry position was near and covered the junction. You could hear what was happening on the other side of the mound. But a mistrustful atmosphere inhabited that end of the trench, and as you got nearer, it was like approaching no man's land, where the enemy could be encountered.

So having the latrine there would not be popular.

"What you fucking digging it there for?"

"We have cleared the location with the section commander," I said.

"Oh, we have, have we? Very posh now, aren't we, cello's friend, and now I suppose friends with this fucker." He indicated the black face of Midnight, who shifted about uncomfortably. "Well, dig it. Go on."

We dug it, having boarded up the old one, while the rest lounged in the bunker, chores supposedly done.

The idleness would surely not last for long.

Midnight had a strange motivation about him, going at his work like a maniac. "You'll tire yourself out, "I said. "You have to keep yourself. Don't use up all your energy in one go. Being a soldier, you need energy in reserve."

"My antecedents were slaves, and they had to be motivated all the time or they got the whip," he said.

I laughed. "Antecedents, what's that supposed to mean."

He stopped and looked at me. "My people, who went before me."

"Oh, I see. Ancestors."

He continued to look at me. "Antecedents are the same. Do you know about slavery?"

"Well, not really, but yes ... I suppose in school, we learned ..." I felt a bit embarrassed.

"Never thought about it much, though, I bet."

"Not really."

"But you can now. With this can't you. I can." He went back to work again.

"Yes, never thought of it like that, but I suppose ..."

"Difference is we get paid. My money goes back to the wife."

"You got a wife?"

"Yes, in Jamaica."

Something hit me in the stomach then, a wife. Midnight was ... well, you couldn't guess his age, being black I had no idea. He was older than me, must 'ave been. I looked at him differently. A family man.

"You're lucky," I said. I just came out with that. Didn't think about it. Then I felt ... to be here, lucky, no. "Well, not lucky to be here and your wife over there, but lucky to have—"

"I am lucky. You should see my wife. She's beautiful, so beautiful. I'll show you a picture later."

I felt ... something, a secret to be shared. It was a kind of privilege. But the others would use it to make fun.

"Would you like to ... you know, with a black girl?"

I suddenly felt a strange twisting between my legs, as if I had been offered something bad at school, but good actually. Some of the men would laugh at that straight out loud in mockery. But I felt that Midnight would not say that to anyone except me. "No ... I ... never thought of it." I laughed. Again I was embarrassed and wanted to say something to make us both laugh, but all I said was, "You, you're a strange one, Midnight." I didn't mean that at all, because saying that kind of drew us apart, but actually I wanted to become better friends and this was a secret that definitely could do that. But instead, we worked on in silence.

Still, this was a sort of look into the future, a different future with a kind of guilty hope. The idea that Midnight and I should somehow share something … almost unheard of, him being from Jamaica, with a wife also black.

I had always thought of myself as ugly, skinny with a thin nose and face. And women … I had no sisters. My mother seemed old even though I was twenty-five but still sort of sheltered. She kept saying I need to get myself married, but then to whom. How to meet someone? There had been some school and town girls. They were always in groups, and I was an outsider in any group of so-called friends, any laughter and giggling were never for me. Mostly I had preferred books. Strange, as we didn't have many books at home, but I got myself to the local library and sat there a lot, when I wasn't at my apprenticeship.

Well, it was a sort of apprenticeship. I knew I wouldn't have it after this. I told Dad once I wanted to be a designer. He laughed right out loud as though he were at the circus watching a clown. He had probably been to the pub. "Designer! And what do you want to design, for gawd's sake?"

"Well …"

"You need to keep your feet on the ground, lad."

He called me lad from when I could remember to when I went away to war. Actually, lad and pal were words used a lot out here. I didn't like them.

Delicate drawings of ships in books had impressed me. I thought I was a little bit good at drawing. "A draughtsman," I announced, feeling a bit grown up using the word.

He mocked it, of course. "Draughtsman! Draughtsman. Ha ha, don't be silly, lad. There'll be fully qualified draughtsmen walking the streets without a farthing in their pocket after this is over."

I am not sure he knew what draughtsmen did.

But then a thought came to me that gave me a small spark of pleasure in my heart. I thought of me walking into our house and behind me was walking a lady, a black lady. And my parents were both in the front room, and they would look up, and the girl would come alongside me and perhaps I would take her hand. Nothing need be said. The look on their faces would say everything. Then before they could start to say and shout what I know would be in their minds, we would turn and leave. We would never go back.

Suddenly we dived. A tiny sound, a far away shout, the parting of air

21

and a rush. Crump. Earth came onto us. We were close together, and I put my hand on top of Midnight helmet to push it further onto his head.

More came over whizz CRUMP. The ground was soft and but not wet. Large sods of mud flew over and dropped into the trench. A large piece of shrapnel hit the trench wall above us and to the right of our new hole for the latrine. "Let's get in there," I shouted to Midnight. We scrambled over the trenching tools and a shovel we had managed to cadge. We dived into the hole we were digging.

"We could be here for some time," commented Midnight. He had a strange way of talking. It was soft and gentle. There was no harshness or swearing and little accent. I did not know what a Jamaican accent should sound like. He seemed almost to speak posh English, as you might hear from an officer. This would be despised by the others. But then we were all a motley crew of various accents and upbringings. We weren't like the Pals battalions from Liverpool or Manchester or the East End of London. We did not have in-jokes or local customs from home that brought us together and comforted us. We were an amalgamated unit. We were from the Worcestershires originally, but the regiment had become so broken by battles from the beginning of the war and lost so many men that any identity had gone as well. So as replacements, we got anybody. Not people from your street or village, instead some musicians from the Artists Rifles, and now a man from Jamaica had joined us.

"Good test for our latrine, Ben, if it's safe from this, then it will make a good one!"

I didn't really have an interest in how safe our latrine was. Though nobody wanted his private parts taken away when he crouching there. It happened, of course. The strangest injuries, deaths, and the survivals happened when men were at their toilet. But if men survived shrapnel stuck in that region of their bodies, when they left the front line, without trousers and adorned by excreta as well as blood and blown off bits, you didn't know whether they would survive. A look into a man's eyes gave you an idea, particularly in response to the inevitable laughter of their colleagues. "I'll come for your misses mate when I'm on leave. You won be needing 'er now," I remember hearing that shout.

Even a young recruit with half a leg blown off might cry for his mother and be terrified. Then you knew he might die. Another with such an injury might wink as he was taken away.

It was the evacuation that every man dreaded. Casualty clearing was either good and fast or it was useless and done by scared no-gooders who were on a charge. The uninjured would beat them as they went by down the trench. It was not usually their fault. How could you protect yourself when you were carrying a stretcher with another man on it? You saw the injury, and you could join that injured man at any moment, or worse, you could be killed outright and he could survive. Why would you want to save him, therefore?

Men hated it, stretcher bearing. But that was what Cello had wanted to do, had done, he said. It was obvious as well afterwards. These were men you fought and died alongside. You gave your life for them, some did, with a generosity that was unexplainable. Some just watched with meanness. How could you lay blame on them, though, even for shooting a casualty?

A strange mixture of things in a man's mind might even lead them to that—a casualty from their own side. Anything is possible. What is life when you cannot live it? You must survive. During the heat of battle, you might kill your own brother if suddenly he came over your trench parapet, bayonet in hand or entrenching tool raised like an executioner's axe. A desperate clash of steel would result.

It might be something entirely innocent, such as the blackness of a man's teeth or the ugliness of them, that made men carelessly smash their rifle into the face. To ensure survival, they had to die. So you would smash it again and again and afterwards joke that you couldn't take the man prisoner because you didn't like his teeth. Death came like a hideous creature, emerging from a need, for your survival. It had different heads that creature. One head gave you your strength; another head was your callousness. That could easily become true for men you didn't know who were evacuated but were going to die. So what? They had a chance but didn't have the strength to take it—better to go then. It was a kind of game of dice; if they died, maybe you would survive. The quota of dead had been satisfied. The same for the casualty in no-man's-land that Jack shot. All he could do was a scream. He didn't deserve to live.

The explosions continued, and we commenced digging through it, taking it in turns to be near the entrance and put the soil out in the main trench. The space gradually got bigger. We started to dig down as well. We didn't talk but often bumped or touched each other or clashed spades.

"Get that fucking bog finished." A shout told us that maybe things had quietened down. Men needed the latrine. When was it not needed? The other one was still being used, but men couldn't stand being in there for more than a moment or two. The disinfectant was so strong it made your eyes stream.

But we couldn't let anyone in until we had dug as deep as possible. Once it had been christened, it filled up fast, and you couldn't make it any deeper.

"It's ours, we built it," said Midnight with a kind of pride.

"Right, let's leave it at that."

"Another few inches deeper, eh," said the maniac Midnight, who was sweating a lot.

"God, you should be the sergeant major." I gave him a playful punch.

"No thanks. Think these people want to get orders from a black fella." That was the first time he referred to his colour.

We eventually collapsed and gave up, shifted the wooden structure from the other latrine, and tied and pegged it onto our one. Then we kind of collapsed together outside the bunker to take water and fags. He brought out a photo, faded and crumpled but clear, and it was clear that the subject, his black wife, was beautiful. She was dressed in a simple dress, and her hair was in waves. It took my breath away. Then he tore of a piece of card from his fag packet and took out the pencil that every soldier was supposed to carry, but most didn't, and wrote an address on it. He handed it to me, and I put it in my pocket with the piece of paper with the address of Cello's parents. I was speechless. I almost cried.

Round the corner of the trench, I heard a briefing for an operation. "Corporal, we will need all your section. Get the men ready for a few days without resup. We'll send some rations and extra water up tonight."

What was this? When would he tell us? You always had to accept, never question. If you did, you would feel the consequences.

Chapter 4

I Want a Coconut
✳ ✳ ✳

That night I was in the bunker. Someone had gone—a tall, lanky streak of "nothing" they called him. I had no idea who he was or what happened to him. Perhaps during the bombardment, he had caught a piece of shrapnel. There seemed to be a lack of togetherness about us. We didn't really care.

"Gettin' a load of extra rations in the morning," I heard the corporal comment.

"Got a little job for us then, Corp?" said Jack.

"You'll hear soon enough."

"Oh, so it is a job."

"Tomorrow; get some rest first."

"Oh, rest is it. Well, must be something entertaining."

The rats began running past and peering in. After a few passes, they would enter and start nosing around the kit. You never left biscuits at ground level in the pack or the equipment. They would dig and rummage until they could drag them out. I lay on my two boards with the cape pulled across them and the blanket on top and listened to them rummaging in someone's pack. It wasn't mine. There was no bombardment and no patrols. We did sentry, Midnight and I, as we had the previous night. It was quiet, and I slept.

Not for long. We were awoken, as in the depot. But with hissed insistence, not shouts. "Get out, get out. We're going. Resupps 'ere. Got to get ready now."

We were up and cramming our packs to bursting with food and ammo, fumbling in the dark as the stuff was thrown at us. How would we carry it all? Then water.

"What about the rum?" asked Jack to no one in particular. He was sleep filled and not his usual sarcastic self.

There was an officer outside. "Rum, rum, not on this trip. I want everybody alert. Let's have you out of there!"

"What are we doing, sir?" someone dared to ask.

"You briefed your men, Corporal?"

"Yes, sir!" came the confident lie.

We looked at each other in the half-light. Any ideas. No questions, shrugs, hands spreading. We didn't know what we were doing, what we had to do.

Confusion trampled on fear as we tried to get ourselves ready. The packs got heavier and heavier, and then came the ammunition. We were grateful for that. We wrapped the canvas bandoliers around us with the clips of rifle ammo. The bandolier contained little canvas pouches, ten I think. Each had two rifle clips of ammo, five rounds. A round was more than a bullet. The bullet was the brown lead tip. Crimped to it was the brass cartridge case containing the explosive and the base. When the firing pin of the rifle hit the base, the explosive went off, firing the bullet. Billions of these were being fired. Millions of them were missing their intended target. Millions were hitting.

The Lewis ammo was already in their circular magazines or still in boxes. You put the circular mags into small rucksacks. An inexperienced gunner would just waste it. Everyone had to carry it, and there were grenades, which we had no room for, but still we found it. Lashed onto packs with extra straps, hanging like a Christmas tree.

We gushed out of the bunker. "Keep quiet, you buggers." There was a sergeant there too. A lieutenant, a sergeant, and two sections of men, maybe ten men and the officer and NCOs. They were already waiting. We came at the end.

We began to make our way along the trench as other men filtered through to take our place in it. We went out at the junction, near the latrine me and Midnight had dug, now forgotten, and scrambled over the top into an old broken sap trench running out towards the Boche positions. We had to wait until there were no flares going up. Each man came over at the same place. In daylight, that would have been mad. We made it, sweating. Then we started crawling along the broken sap. The noise seemed unbearably loud. A single file is a snake of men, but you are not in contact with the head or tail. You are in a bubble, on your own, waiting to hear something from the ends. Well not waiting, coz you are moving or taking cover or … doing whatever everyone else is doing. You are like a small ant moving as they do, in a file, except they probably know more about what is going on.

Crawling with everything is the hardest thing. Bandoliers get caught. They get full of earth and mud. You keep your hands up holding your weapon not on the ground where there's old wire and maybe unexploded ammo and much else besides, unmentionable things. Things you would never talk about in a letter home. I thought of letters home as letters to Cello's mother, not to mine. That place was a blank. It's the elbows and forearms that are used to work you forward over these unmentionable things—and your knees, of course. In the dark, what you didn't notice you didn't care about, not so much.

It was clear to me that we were going towards the same temporary trench we had occupied when the Cello incident occurred. Then there seemed to be only a few of us. Now we had more strength. But we couldn't talk. Our noise was enough to alert the enemy anyway, I thought, and I waited for the moment when all hell would come down on our heads.

We crawled and inched forward. You thought about something that hurt your shoulders or whether stuff was coming out of the pouches on the sides and front of your gear. The rifle might get blocked with mud. You worried about this.

"Fix bayonets!" a hissed whisper came back. I reached for the long blade, sharp enough to pierce a man's uniform and even the straps on his equipment. When forcing it, you always tried to miss any metal that he might be wearing, like a belt of ammunition. Hesitate and he could brush it aside. You could cut his arm in the process, but killing was not an easy thing with the bayonet. Which was why some men used the trenching tool. You got mad enough to use any heavy instrument, blunt or sharp.

I was still fumbling for my bayonet. What a silly bastard, not to have it ready. The straps hurt and twisted, but I got it out with some exertion and tried silently to fix it. Oil was needed to make that as quiet as possible.

That was how they often got you on inspection. "Okay, remove the bayonet … ahh, no oil on the handle. Can't get it off, eh lad? Well, you had better get more practice. Two hours extra bayonet drill for this man, Corporal."

"Very good, sir."

I got it on the rifle and sank back down in the mud. Why had we not done this before setting off? Must be getting near something, something. I tried to remember the layout of the trench as I shuffled forward. I closed my eyes to try to picture it.

"Wire here." A harsh whisper awoke me, sort of. Where was the wire, high or low? In the dim light, I could see a bit of an entanglement running above the sap, which here was little more than a scrape. As if some careless giant had dragged his boot heel through the mud and created it. Thankfully he had dragged out most of the more horrific debris of war. We hadn't had too many bodies to crawl through. Literally crawl through, I mean. Sometimes you could find yourself putting your hands into a man's stomach as you moved in no man's land. Gloves were almost as prized as boots in the trenches, but as the weather warmed, requests home for them seemed increasingly ignored.

We were moving more freely now, scraping along the scrape. Hearts were still pounding, and earth penetrated every bit of uniform and equipment. But we were getting used to the motion and more confident since our presence did not seem to have roused the Boche, though we were getting closer to his positions, so we should not have been gaining confidence.

Then, after an age, it seemed painful to move as we tumbled one after another into a deeper trench. The lieutenant in front had found the way into it. I thanked him silently for this refuge. It was now black, as any night could be, and we all just lay listening for any sound indicating that we had disturbed the balance of the night in no man's land, where men's souls were visible even though men weren't. In an instant, my mind went back to the song we sang before they shot Cello.

Out of the night that covers
Me,
Black as the pit from pole to
Pole.
I thank whatever gods may
Be
For my unconquerable soul.

But mine was a shattered soul, shattered and black as the night itself. I saw Midnight's shining face. A black man but somehow not pitch black, whatever that was, a coal mine, I suppose. I could sleep here, here and now. We huddled together. *What are we doing here?* was my final thought as we drifted into a kind of stupor. I saw Cello's house, and I had to get to it down a cliff or winding road, and when I got there, I crawled in through the window, and there was nothing there and no one. Cello was somewhere at the back of me or in my mind. I could feel his presence, but of course, he wasn't there.

We did sleep, because it was still night, and we just stayed where we were, bunched together in an unsoldierly fashion. One shell would have done for us all. I think we were waiting for the lieutenant to decide something, so the responsibility was taken away from us. No one told us anything, so we didn't do anything. But we did pass around the sentry duty, shaking each other every hour. "You're on, mate. Stay awake, for gawd's sake." The hour of duty got shorter and shorter. "You're on now."

"What, again?"

"Just do it."

The dawn light stole up without us noticing as it does; grey, always grey, coming from nowhere to wake an exhausted world, shy and dreading what will be revealed and wanting only to inhabit the dark. Why did we bother again to wake?

We were like giant slugs, earth-encrusted, slimed with soil and the blood of the soil but not caring. When our eyes could focus on each other's eyes, they saw holes, like those of the latrines, where darkness and foulness lurked, and men's souls had departed to hibernate from the light, from truth, from reality, from fear.

Movement was minimal, but each knew that the other was there and awake and alive. The stillness of a dead man comes from a lack of breath and a still heart—when you are waiting for that breath, the heart moves the body as much as the limbs of the running man. We waited to hear sounds of the Boche trenches.

We became aware of a more solid shelter towards the direction we were travelling when we stopped. It was a bunker, perhaps German, perhaps ours. We needed to get inside it. But the lieutenant would be checking it in daylight, such daylight as there was. It might have been occupied or booby trapped. It might have been full of water or shit, definitely that, and rats and ammunition and the dead, grinning to greet us.

But then a body half rose ahead of us, and an arm beckoned. The slugs began to move, slug-like.

A screeching split the air, like an express train out of control, making our need for silence suddenly meaningless. It was a bombardment, and it was heavy. At that moment when shells were in the air, you didn't know if they were ours or theirs. The artillery shell is a lazy creature. He goes up, so, so high. Who knows how high? Even in summer, the joke would be "They'll have snow on them when they land." But where do they land, and whom do they bother to shed their shrapnel on, blast their shrapnel into? The soft tissue, the bones, the brains, the men made of clay, the clay churned into mush by the laughing, lazy artillery.

Taking advantage of the noise, we scrambled onwards, not caring what horror greeted us in the bunker, wanting only to get away from the bombardment, then tumbled into the bunker as the shells began to land and the noise, at first like the slamming of a heavy door in an empty house, repeated and repeated, then immediately merged into a shaking, battering devastation and thunder, which could make hell jealous, and the screaming of more shells merged with the slamming and the thunder and then the chunks of shrapnel came and the sods of clay flying and flung. But we didn't look up and hid in a heap of bodies, suddenly elated to be safe, partly elated as if in temporary respite from the monster retribution.

It was ours and aimed at the German trenches. So we could assess that the guns were trying to breach the wire that lay between us and the Boche trenches.

One of our section put his head up with an awful mud-stained grin. "They supporting us. They doing this for us, ain't they?"

"No, mate. This is not for us. We been forgotten, this is for the next show."

"What we doing here then?"

"Nobody knows!"

Then he started screaming and crying. "What we doing? I want to know. I don't want them coming here and thinking we's the Boche. They'll do that won they."

"No, they won't do that," I said.

"How do you know? You are a fucking traitor, ain't you?" As if I had deliberately brought these men here so they could be killed by our own people.

We all had wild thoughts, wanting to blame somebody. I just looked away from Jack, but I knew most of them were on his side, trying to scapegoat me. If there were any heroics required, I would be the one forced out to do something.

Eyes coming out from under helmets had bayonets on them. Mud, eyes, the stench and the noise—these made up our fearful world of the moment. The souls had departed behind the eyes, way behind.

"Men," the officer's voice rose above the screaming, rumbling, banging, and shaking of the shells, "when this finishes, we are going to do a raid on the German trench. We want to take some things back, to test them out. Find out about their morale and stuff. I want you all to get something, just get something, and then we withdraw."

What sort of a plan was this! Men looked at each other. It sounded like school playground stuff. Or the sort of thing the officers would come up with after dinner in the mess, hooting with laughter. I thought of the truckload of officers that had almost run me down after they shot Cello, singing as they headed into town, driven into town singing. This war was sometimes so stupid and senseless and mean, where tiny things became massive and massive things, like the shooting of an innocent man, were tiny and insignificant.

It stopped. The last scream fading into a death, perhaps an unexploded shell lying in wait for us, too lazy to blow us to kingdom come.

Someone did start praying then. "Our father, who art in heaven ..."

One of the slugs moved. "Shut it, you booger."

The tone heralded a little lightness. What else could they do, only laugh in a grisly way? "Yeah, that *our father* ain't seen his fucking artillery."

"Is 'e on our side?"

"Course, we's English, ain't we?" Then there was laughter, shaking the slugs. It was relief at the stopping of the bombardment. And it was nervous anticipation at what might come, a mad rushing of the German trenches in broad daylight. It was a moment that lifted the soul or helped restore a kind of shared one.

A grey hand went up. "Be quiet now. We are not going in daylight. We will go this evening, perhaps when they are resting and feeding."

Was this someone talking sense, someone thinking for once.

We didn't have time to wait for evening. They came at us straight after the bombardment. They must have known we were there. Stupid to think we could get away with it. Fortunately for me and the others that got away, they came from the other sap on the other side of the bunker from the way we had come. And we heard them as well. A shout, maybe nervous, and the sound of equipment and bodies on the soil. The lieutenant was first out of our bunker, and he shot two with his revolver. I think he was on his knees when I ran out and turned right into the sap where we had slept. Then I bounded up the far bank a few steps. I turned and sat back on the bank of the sap bringing my rifle across me. Being left-handed was good because they had gone to ground at the bottom of the sap looking forward towards our bunker but not up to the left, and being mostly right-handed, their left eyes would be kind of closed, and their helmets tilted when they took aim, and I was behind their helmet. I squeezed off the safety catch. I was amazingly calm. I shot a couple that was trying to take aim after the officer shot the two in front.

Most of the men had come out of the bunker. "Get back, back down the sap!" I yelled. Most men were just stumbling around, trying to run, withdraw, as it would be called on some official report. Some turned and loosed off a round or two. They weren't aimed shots. Midnight saw me and followed me, not them. He actually went higher up the bank so he could get a better position. He was right-handed. He started shooting.

We killed all of them visible in the sap. It was only then that I started to think of Cello and the casualty we shot. But these, I liked shooting them. There were more coming. "Time to go," Midnight shouted.

I dropped to the bottom of the sap. The others were almost out of sight, scuttling like rats. I half-turned to look where Midnight was. Something like a sledgehammer caught me in the. I didn't know where it was. A flash blinded me. The explosion was inside my head. Then nothing.

Midnight literally dragged me out.

Apparently, we had become heroes. But we had a long way to go. I couldn't help thinking about Cello's casualty as we were going, dragging, scrambling back to our own trench. I was bleeding like hell, and my equipment was holding my stomach together. I felt a terrible heat spreading down my paralysed left side and across my stomach. My arms tried to help Midnight. Dragging handfuls of mud, clawing and crawling. One leg was sort of working.

They didn't come after us. They had their fucking bunker back. But it was expensive for them. Perhaps six dead or badly injured. It seemed we had lost only the officer. He died for us.

The pain increased as my movement slowed. Very soon I could do nothing to help Midnight. I was a dead weight. I daren't look at my stomach. I wouldn't be able to see it anyway; it was covered in my equipment, still holding everything together, with my uniform, covered in mud and blood and having more blood pumped out of it. My left hand was free and dragging lifelessly; I didn't know why. Had I been hit in the shoulder as well? Everything on my left side was a mass of numbness and immobility, on the outside at least. On the inside, it was different. If you don't feel anything in your stomach, that usually means everything is working normally. When it isn't, you soon know about it. I felt now as though I had swallowed a rock, a huge one, and it was burning.

Somehow we got back to the trench. At the end, I didn't know who helped or how I got there. At one point I shouted to leave me; the pain was too great. They didn't leave me. Yes, others had come to help Midnight. Or we had caught up with them. I didn't know which. The shouts and the exertion and the explosions were like something from another world, a drunken one perhaps. I had almost passed out from drink once when we had our first night off during our infantry training in England. The room had spun, and the floor seemed an uncertain place. This was one hundred times worse. I needed to drink and vomit at the same time.

The desperation for a drink was uppermost. I tried to reach for men's water bottles. I focused on that one thing. I could eat the bottle and break the liquid out from it like a coconut with its milk impossibly sealed inside its hairy exterior. I had tasted it once at a fairground, after my father, in desperation to win one, had spent all his money and eventually reaped the dubious reward. I had no idea why I should think of that at this time. My mind was out of my head, just as my stomach was trying to get out of its lining, was out already. I was dying. I wished it would get dark and perhaps my craving for a drink would pass. No one gave me water. Eventually, someone encased my middle area in dressings, mummy-like.

I wanted the dark to come. Everything was so slow. My body had stopped functioning, but my mind wandered listlessly on. My hearing, although working, did not penetrate the pain to make any sense.

Any movement meant intense pain. I screamed, "STOP, YOU BUGGEEEEERS," something like that.

I cried tears of pain.

There was a bouncing which was terrible. I was on a stretcher. It made me want to die more.

There were jokes in the trenches constantly about the surgeons who treated the injured. And about wooden legs and arms, they made you look like a puppet, which never worked. One day someone had come up with the wooden head joke. A surgeon had created a wooden head so that men who had they're original blown off could be fitted with it and returned to the front lines.

But experiencing the medical care as I did made me think that I was in the hands of angels. They gently removed my equipment, cut away the uniform and dressings, and started work straight away. I must have been very close to the lines. We reached the first dressing station quickly, and it seemed as though I was in another world straight away, one that would look after me. I relaxed and drifted. Perhaps they had given me something for the pain—yes, morphine, that was it. I drifted more, but wanted to hang onto this listlessness, for the pain had been so great that I feared its return if the morphine wore off, as in childhood you fear sleep lest the return of some nightmare.

Apparently, they found heavy damage to my spleen, liver, stomach, and kidneys. It must have been a grenade. But there was no enemy close to us. They didn't need to do a laparotomy, or an operation to open up my belly. It was already shredded. All they had to do was open the flaps, like torn cardboard, and work on the organs within. They stitched them up and got me out, to make way for all the others in the queue. Others who no doubt had injuries worse than mine.

As I slowly awoke—hours, it might have been days—later, I thought I was whole again. But I was like a leaky bag, done up with rotten string. My long-term problems were only just beginning.

I was taken out of the front line dressing station on a horsedrawn cart and then transferred to a lorry, bumping and grinding through endless roads and ways. We were three deep in racks of stretchers. I was in the middle. The man above me couldn't keep still. I think he was dead by the time we reached wherever we were going. His screaming had stopped anyway. We all bled. But his bleeding, which had become a steady stream onto me, had stopped by the end of the journey. I started bleeding again at the first bump, I think. No one tended to our injuries during the journey. Only the driver cursed onwards. It was stifling as we were inside a box.

A man could believe he was on his own in such a box, with no knowledge of where he was going or how long it would take to get there. But in fact, there must have been fleets and fleets of such vehicles heading back from the front, all with injured and dying men in them, all in agony. Some might be wretched sort of malingerers, although they wouldn't be given the luxury of an ambulance. *Luxury.* "OH GOD. DRIVER, LET US OUT TO PISS." That was me. There was a small metal grill that gave access to the driver's cab for shouts. He was, of course, oblivious to the screams of pain.

The driver cursed on. "SHUT THE FUCK UP," he shouted.

A thought came to my mind that he might shoot us if we stopped.

"Let us out to die then you bastard."

"Can't stop for nuttin. I got ambulances ahead, ambulances behind. We just in a convoy, going back to the corps area. If you gonna die, then die quietly, if you don mind."

"Going back to the corps area." That took me back to the court-martial centre and Cello. But surely we were going further back than that. We kept going and going.

I pissed myself. But then I thought it must have been blood. There was no ending of the stream and no grateful shaking to ensure the drops didn't go down your trousers. Everything down there was a mess, and a dull ache as pain tablets wore off. I wanted to smoke. The others did as well, but we would have all choked to death, which might also have dulled the pain and been a better way to go.

I slept and dreamt horribly trying to wake myself as I thought I was dying. When I did awake, I was soaked in perspiration as well as blood and urine. There was no shit though that was the one bodily function I had not yet done, and I thought I might never again do with the mess I was in.

We did reach a destination, but it was only a temporary halt for me. I was inspected. I heard mumblings, but one word did come through the haze of the new dose of pain tablets. "Infection."

A hasty conference was held. Out of all the casualties, why was I given this treatment? Stained white coats around me. A red cross apron and a tall figure with it. Cello. He had had such an apron. I relaxed knowing I was in good hands. But it was a woman, not Cello.

She spoke to me. It seemed as though it had been forever since anyone had done that. Before I had been a piece of meat. Now I was a person again. "Hello, young man, Benjamin isn't it? I am Doctor Finch. You have some infection in your stomach wounds, and so we would rather not treat you here in France. We are sending you to a hospital ship which is currently docked in Calais, and you will sail tomorrow for England. Here are some pain tablets for you to take whenever you need. I have put your possessions in a haversack with your stretcher. We hope you have a safe journey and a good recovery."

ENGLAND. I hardly heard any more. YOU ARE ONE OF THE LUCKY ONES. Yes, finally some luck had come my way.

The drugs did their work. I knew nothing.

Chapter 5

I Get a Bag for Life

✳ ✳ ✳

The lucky ones. This thought and the way we were thus branded would make me and many others bitter over the course of the next months and years and decades. It resounded like a church bell. We weren't the unclean, like some who returned whole but with venereal diseases. We weren't the dead who had been left in France. We weren't the broken ones who returned with stuttering mouths, darting eyes and shaking hands. Oh no, we were the lucky ones. We might not have to return again. We might be here for the rest of the war—and then some. A few sick years in institutions, doing what the rules said and taking whatever pity was doled out.

Here, where we landed eventually, not knowing where but knowing that it was for a time, possibly a long one. With a stomach wound, there was no respite, which men got from drinking and eating. Everything came through a drip at first. Only smoking was some relief.

NO SMOKING, IN BED, ON THE WARDS. This was a sign behind every bed and was usually the first subject of conversation when you were able to make conversation, which many couldn't, as their faces had been all but blown away. But they still wanted to smoke, through some hole in the ghastly mask that once had been their face. But the staff took the sign as meaning that there was no smoking in bed or on the wards, which was pretty final for those that couldn't get out of bed. But the beds could be pushed on their wheels, and if you could get out of the confines of the ward, into the corridor that ran alongside the windows, you were okay. So eventually when we found the strength to manoeuvre the beds ourselves, along the wall and out. We could smoke because the sign said we couldn't smoke in bed on the ward, which implied that we could smoke in bed off the ward.

Some nurses allowed it. Some allowed themselves to be kissed. That fortune never befell me.

Woolwich was where we were. A hospital with long, long wards and corridors and beds where each man lived out his own private hell.

Lucky ones? Never. We had come by hospital ship to Woolwich docks and been driven off the short distance to this place. The only good thing that you could say was that the transportation was a lot better than that first journey from the front line. And each move gave you a little bit of renewed hope. But once here, the final destination, you realised that maybe it was final.

A hospital shows what war is, I decided. The sights and sounds of the most horrific injuries and the casual chance of the arrival of death was merely an extension of the trenches, but with people in stiff starched white aprons. At night, well, that was when the real, utterly lonely pain of each man came out, in screams and sobs and thrashing around in dreams, each one revisiting some terrible moment, some private guilt or some fear. Then, of course, the pain was always worst at night, when you couldn't get comfortable and you knew there wouldn't be any pain relief probably till morning, when someone else perhaps had been taken from his bed, the silent ritual of the dead.

I got gangrene. It was deep inside my intestines, probably in the colon, I was told. Everything around my belly area was a welter of stinking blue-black flesh.

"They got special maggots for that," someone wisely pointed out. There was always a wise patient who loved to be the purveyor of bad news. He didn't seem to die or ever have real pain. He just lay there revelling in the agony of others.

It was true, though. But I would not get the maggot treatment.

"You'd be okay if it were yer leg. They'd just chop it off. Then you definitely wouldn't be going back." To the trenches, he meant, of course. Almost every piece of conversation was about going back, not going home.

"Don't you be too sure. They got such good wooden legs now. They'll probably pass you fit when you got one. Then you definitely go back.

"Yea, they dress you in uniform, so it covers everything. Just stand you there and look at you, then call out 'Number such and such, yeah, he's fit, A1. Back you go.'"

"Still, they can't chop off yer stomach, can they? Where you say it was?"

"Colon."

"Yeah, I know. You'll have to have a bag, to piss and shit in like. Tied around yer waist, rest of yer life, mate."

"You lucky bastard. That'll definitely keep you out of going back."

"But the bag'll be inside yer uniform, won't it? So you still be passed as fit as well."

"Won't even put you up there, not with one of those things."

"Does it stink? You know, when it's got shit inside it?" I asked stupidly.

The conversation stopped abruptly from the two men in beds opposite. After a thoughtful pause, one said, "Well, it would, wouldn't it? I mean, who wants to carry around a bag of their own shit with them?"

Men were dying daily. Some had most of their faces blown off. Others had lost both legs and were lying in bed like babies with just the top of their bodies making a lump in the bedclothes. But somehow the idea of carrying around a bag of your own shit for the rest of your life was more repulsive at that moment than all these things.

I sweated with the pain. Before that, I had started to eat a little, but now as soon as I did, I became sick and vomited. I had started to walk to the toilet. I couldn't anymore. I had to do it into a bedpan, and I saw the blood in it immediately.

Surgeons came and said they would have to operate.

Would I live? The exhausted doctor didn't seem to know. He would try. I would have a stoma.

What was it?

"Part of your bowel has died through lack of blood. Probably after being twisted in the initial operation, done just after you were wounded. Now we have to take that away and divert all waste products out of your intestine."

They always tried to conceal the bad news with technical detail. "Will I have a bag?"

"You will have a colostomy?"

"What is a colostomy?"

"Yes, it's a receptacle for waste."

After the operation, I just lay there for a long time. Nurses came and went. They did something to me, presumably changing the bag. They were amazing, and their hands were comforting. That was my only comfort. At night I dreamt. They were confusing dreams at first about trenches, and the pain and the desire to drink and coconuts and having a shit in no man's land. A boche sniper was shooting up my arse.

Then I started dreaming of someone. It was midnight. Then he was dying, not me, but I couldn't save him.

Then I started having dreams in the day. Someone said it was a "flashback".

Then I saw Cello. He was as clear as daylight, in the early morning, while the sun was still just rising. He was coming over the top of the trench, smiling in a crooked kind of way. That ridiculous apron. A Red Cross one had been given to him by the Germans. It had mud on it, no blood, just mud. He came smiling, and then he came again, again, not talking. Again he came.

I awoke sweating. The paper, his parents' address, and Midnight's wife's address, my things. These were the only things worth keeping.

The morning round of nurses came. I grabbed a hand. "Was there anything that came with me, any stuff, my uniform, in the pocket?"

"We keep everything that comes with the patients. We know how important it can be."

"WHERE?"

"I will look."

She returned like an angel bearing something, a small canvas bag, very small. "These are the only personal effects. Everything else was army issue."

"What's inside?"

"Wait a minute." The canvas bag which was tied up with a piece of waxed string. There was a label on the outside, on which was written, "54698760 Private Benjamin John Routledge."

"That is your name, isn't it?"

"Yes," I said automatically, impatiently.

"Well, let's look inside."

I was sweating. The bag seemed nothing, to contain nothing. It was flat. There was no depth to it. She opened it and looked inside, then looked at me with slight pain.

"Well?"

"Wait a minute." She opened the bag a little more. "Ahh." She put her fingers and extracted a grey piece of shrapnel and a bullet. "This must have been what did the damage to you."

I looked at it incredulously. "What on earth. Why would they … ?"

"Some men like to know what it was that caused their pain; otherwise, how do they know that the thing is not still inside them?"

I was speechless. The only thing I could think about was my mother holding one of my baby teeth. That was in another life, nothing to do with this …

Then my head dropped back. I was exhausted, and a deep hurt began to take hold of my heart.

"Sorry, no there is something else," I heard her say. This time my heart leapt. "Is this what you wanted?"

I raised my head. She was holding a piece of paper. Then she slid her fingers apart. It was two pieces of paper.

"Yes," I heard myself say. I was mechanical, like a dead man who had come back to life. I felt nothing at first. Then I experienced a feeling of relief that I had never known before. It was a kind of ending and beginning. For some reason, I thought of God. I reached my hand out, and she put these scraps, which had become a kind of treasure, into it.

The papers were unmistakable. Cello's one was more worn but just readable. Midnight's was better, being cardboard.

Suddenly I was sweating again. They were so vulnerable and fragile. I would lose them. I read them, and for the first time since I could remember, I almost laughed. Midnight was there with me. Cello was not, and that made my heart ache. He was my friend that never was, even though he had chosen me as his court-martial friend. He saw something in me that I didn't see myself. He gave me a duty and mission.

As yet I didn't know what that was to be.

I looked at the nurse, still standing there. "How did it manage to be kept?"

"As I said we do take care of soldier's effects. We do that well, I think."

41

"Christ, you do. That is my future." I knew this to be true. "Please put them back and keep them safe. I will need them."

She put the pieces of paper back in the bag and resealed it. "We will keep them safe, under lock and key until you are ready for them. That is going to be soon."

"I don't know about that, but I am hoping."

"What about the bullet and shrapnel?" She asked.

"You have plenty of rubbish bins put it in one of them. I never want to see that again."

Chapter 6

I Write Two Letters
✳ ✳ ✳

I was moved to a ward where men were recovering. The summer had disappeared without notice.

I had not been well enough to write a letter to my parents, but the War Office, who sent out the telegrams informing next of kin about deaths and informing them of other things, had written to them, telling them of my final destination. They eventually made the long journey to see me.

"How are you, lad?" asked my father awkwardly, on arriving at the bed. My mother, walking behind, had a ridiculous hat and coat on, which I could never have imagined them affording. They must have argued endlessly about their purchase. But here they were. She smiled slightly, obviously relieved that they had made it to my bedside without too much embarrassment. There was no sign of affection except a placing of a gloved hand on my arm, over the bedclothes.

"So good to see you, Benjamin. How are you?" she said.

At that moment a gulf had opened, which was impossible to explain or bridge. Oceans and torrents passed down it, with soldiers marching into it as though in a joyful suicide into the sea. Rivers of blood with bodies floating, seas of mud with men and horses drowning in it, a landslide where all the stories of soldiers, became ugly and grotesquely twisted, like the ugly twisting trenches and bunkers where we tried to live a miserable existence around stinking latrines and punishments and firing squads and bombardments and red crosses and hospital beds with groaning corpses of the half-dead; flowed down the torrent unheeded, unnoticed by my mother and father. They reached across it without noticing. They stepped over it without comment. They stepped gingerly in a new coat and hat with gloves even. Perhaps they didn't want to touch the reality. Who could even start to show them? Don't look down now, Mother, Father, don't stare into the abyss. What does it mean? What in the name of everything does it mean?

Who could know? How could all our culture and everything we had known be lost in those torrents, in the streams of blood being poured out? How was it that here half-sitting were my parents and, like the parent of every human being, they tried in whatever way they could to bring their offspring into a life based on the understanding of certain things about their own lives, wrestling with good and bad and hoping for a good boy or girl, rejoicing in an enrichment of the offspring's life. So how could it be possible that the world, consisting of people who were also parents, allowed these torrents to happen? How senseless it was to tell, think, or try to write a letter, anything to parents about these things.

"I'm … as well as they can make me I suppose," I said. I felt inclined to pile on the agony and tell them everything about my condition. But what would it matter? What would be the point? They wouldn't understand, and it would seem as though I was making more of my situation, whereas everybody knew …

"You're lucky to get out of it, eh?" said my father, taking the words right out of my head.

"Yes, lucky," I replied.

"Are you in pain a lot, Benjamin?" my mother asked. It was strange to hear my full first name. They had seen a ward sister who told them in a kind of listless way of my injuries and my result, a bowel bag for the rest of my life and ongoing treatment for my internal and external injuries.

All from one stray bullet or grenade or both somehow.

The hospital had its usual smell of disinfectant, the fluid used for injections and polished floors. My mother seemed to go with the smell. Although perhaps she should have had a white coat instead of the grey-green one. Still, she seemed unusually clean from what I remember. But then after life in the trenches, anything was clean, and anything associated with a former home would never be the same again.

"Well … lad." My father was lost for words and looked around, searching for a way out. "We'll come and see you again."

"Yes, of course, Benjamin." My mother was an unlikely echo and seemed not to believe herself. Perhaps they thought I would be in the hospital forever. Perhaps that was the punishment for being "lucky".

They left as embarrassed as they had arrived and I lay back gratefully, but then a huge loneliness swept over me. It came on as relief, and I didn't realise until much later that it was loneliness. Just as a teenager growing up craves independence, an injured man craves company and understanding of that injury, without having to explain it. Or he wants to talk about it and explain it over and over. But I noticed that the other men who loved to talk of their injuries to each other, or more often talk of another's injury and pontificate over it when he was not in earshot, also fell strangely silent when families including wives in some cases, were visiting.

I really was lucky though. My fear of the future became replaced by some hope of making contact with the families associated with Cello and Midnight. I thought of them as a real family. They replaced my family, because they had a kind of secret link to our life in the trenches. I didn't then realise that Cello's family would see me as taking part in the shooting of their son. Even worse, I didn't realise that they would see part of my duty as righting the wrong of his death. I thought they would be on my side. I never thought differently.

I was a coward, and I was arrogant.

I had operations. I got better at dealing with my "shit bag", as the others in the ward called it. It was also other organs that gave me huge problems, but I was up and about more, though constantly bent almost double with pain.

The improvement was enough to encourage remarks from others. "They'll be looking to get you back out there, mate. You'll see. Got your uniform there awready." He pointed at the brand-new uniform hanging on the hook behind the bed. I was in pyjamas most of the time. The army also provided those, laundered once a week. Soon they would encourage me to get dressed, and there was only one set of clothes in which to dress. The army held you in its grip. Just as when I had gone to be Cello's friend for the court-martial, the army was waiting, knowing my every move. Here again, they were waiting.

I tried to tear myself away, to focus on a future. There was a library, which seemed deserted most of the time. It had been a ward. Now the beds were replaced by shelves of dead books. It had a small writing table and chair but was not warm enough to in sit for long bouts of reading or letter writing, which was what I wanted to do. It was autumn now, getting towards winter, and the army did not run to issuing out dressing gowns. If you had a personal coat, so much the better. My parents did not think to bring such an article. They never came back to see me, although they did write to say they were trying to get money for the train fare. So I had to wrap myself in an army blanket.

We eventually got a little money from our army pay. It was a few pounds a month, paid by "the paymaster" or his assistant, an overweight captain with a moustache that would have looked better on a general. Pay parade was a funny affair. We didn't have to wear a uniform, although some struggled to do so. In the centre of the ward a table was set, not with a tablecloth or anything, just a plain table, and we assembled around it. Then someone told us to line up. Usually the senior man present. We were like a military unit. "Number 2S ward, WARRRRD, SHUN!" There was a shuffling. Fortunately, no inspection was done. The paymaster's assistant breezed in with a boxful of brown envelopes. He stood at the table behind us. Then the order was given. "Number 2S ward, ABOUUUUT TURN!" More shuffling until we faced the paymaster's assistant. He eyed us with very small eyes as if trying to assess whether we had earned our money. Of course, we had not. Perhaps he was a spy for the medical board, to which we would all need to report at some time.

The orderly, who was always a nurse, sometimes male, helped him with his boxes of envelopes, which were then turned around to face the paymaster. He took the first envelope and called out its name. The soldier in question would answer, "Here, sir." Then he would march forward and present his paybook to the officer. Our paybooks had been given to us once they had followed us to the hospital from wherever the pay office of our particular regiment was based. The officer would pass over the small brown envelope and make a note in the paybook to that effect. The man would withdraw.

One month, or it may have happened on more than one occasion, the officer had brought the wrong envelopes. This did not become clear until at least three names had been read out and failed to be claimed by anyone. "Baldini ... Battenhouse ... Bloomberg." Names were always called in alphabetical order. But these names sounded like the cast of some silent horror moving a picture or comic book, not real people. They must have been cases from the mental ward. We asked the nurses about that and tried to listen to the pitiful night-time cries of these cases whose brains had been torn apart and would remain in the mental state of infants for the rest of their lives. Back in our ward we listened to the autumn wind and tried to distinguish it from the dream induced moans of these creatures.

We also had our own dreams, nightmares, and flashbacks.

The only subject of conversation after the pay parade was how it came to be that most of us got different amounts of money in our envelopes. "What did you get, Ben?"

"Nineteen shillings and threepence ... you?"

"I topped you this month. One pound, ten shillings, and fourpence."

"You got one whole pound! You lucky bugger. The extra fags are on you."

We shuffled out onto the balcony for a smoke. We didn't question or look into why these sums differed. Some said it was tax, some sent money home to a wife. Some had moved regiments and their money hadn't caught up with them. In any event, the basic for a private, to which we all reverted to once injured, was one shilling and one penny per day. War pay now gave extra if you were on the front line, and this was to some an incentive to get back. But others said it was coffin money and wouldn't have it. We had to pay for fags from our measly money. In the trenches, some fags came with the rations. So did rum. But here rum or any alcohol was as rare as, well, rocking horse shit, as some put it.

I could not write to Cello's parents or to Midnight's wife on the flimsy army form letters that were issued out, complete with pencil. So I had to buy some fancy notepaper and envelopes. I needed a pen as well. But I would get free postage, up to a certain weight. The soldier who wanted to do something different, even though he was in the hospital, was not catered for. Even going to the library made me a figure of fun. "Going back to school again, Ben? Forget it. Can readin' books stop this lot? No way!"

I got a nurse to go out and get the notepaper and envelopes. I retired to the library, not to read as some thought but to write. Wrapped in an army blanket, I started my first letter.

The Royal Herbert Hospital

Shooters Hill
Woolwich
London
28 October 1917

Dear Sir and Madam (I decided that they must be well educated, being the parents of a cellist)

I would like to introduce myself to you. I am Private Benjamin Routledge.

I write from my hospital bed having been wounded in action in France.

I am a friend of your son. I am sorry that he didn't come back (I had no idea what they would have been told about his demise). I know he was a musician, a cello player. His loss is deeply felt by you, I have no doubt at all of that.

As his friend, I feel his loss and sadness that I didn't know him better.

He was a good man. I can tell you that because I know.

I would like to try and get some leave to come and visit you. When I get a bit better. I don't know when but if this would be of consideration to you in a favourable way then I would be happy and make all efforts to visit.

I remain your faithful servant, (I had seen this somewhere in a business letter and thought it sounded grand and might impress them. Though I failed to notice that I could hardly remain their faithful servant when I not yet become such).

BENJAMIN

I looked down at my hands after writing it. The middle of the fingers

48

was yellow from tobacco. The ends of the fingers were white and almost transparent, and yet around the nails, the stain of trench dirt could be seen. God, it was five months since I had left the trenches, since my hands had clawed desperately at the mud in that sap that Midnight had dragged me down, to safety.

I began to shake a little. We had seen these sorts of hands on our fellow patients. It was one of the signs of oncoming death, of the body giving up the fight.

I clenched and unclenched the hands and shook them to try to get some blood back into them. When you are lying in bed with your body giving up, you fight for your heart, not your hands. You forget them. Drips are feeding you, and you don't need them. The writing of the letters brought them back to me. I needed them.

I sealed the letter shakily having read and reread it so many times holding it in my stained fingers that I thought it would be so dirty they would think it was a fake.

I asked a nurse to send it, as I didn't trust the normal mail delivery service, which probably censored all the letters. I didn't want that. I trusted the nurse.

As soon as I had written the letter, I felt better. I had a reason to get better. Then I began to contemplate the next letter. I could not pin my hopes on one letter. Two would give me more chance of a reply.

This one was different. I could not get the woman's beauty out of my mind. Midnight was a man who had saved my life. I wanted to meet him again. I wanted him to be able to go back to his wife and family. Still, there was a nagging thought of secrecy in my mind. Then another thought, was it right to write to his wife without his permission? I dismissed that thought straight away. That little scrap of paper with its address was the only way of getting back to him. If that was through his wife, so be it. I would need to word the letter in such a way that would not make her, or him if he got to see it, suspicious. This, in a way, made the secrecy more, well … exciting. Until I sat down to write the letter.

Then I was filled with dread, and my arm was like stone. The trenches came flooding back—the shouting, the mud in the face, the fear of the grey-uniformed hun teeming into our hideaway. Then a little short-lived elation as I shot a couple with my left-handed advantage. Even right-handed

I would have had an advantage, but getting into position would have been more difficult, and I might not have thought of doing it from where I was on the bank. Anyway, it was to no avail. After that there was nothing but agony and Midnight, dragging me.

Life is made of moments.

In between was a sea of regret—of tiny sights, sounds, and smells that stuck, like a snapped branch sticking, splintered from mud without its parent tree in sight. On the way back up to the front after Cello's court-martial, there were so many things partially hidden in the mud alongside the paths packed hard by ours and many other boots. There was the horror of stepping off the path to an unknowing death, watched by the thousand mile stare of others who moved on in a blind procession.

A soldier's actions were automatic, not predictable or controlled. They moved not so much to an order, although often that did happen. But as a reaction to an event, spread by a word of one man, or without a word, such as when gas appeared, yellow, floating. You could duck beneath it or stand up above it and get your head taken off by shrapnel. The reaction was automatic, the result totally unpredictable and in most cases arbitrary.

The shooting of the casualty which led to Cello's action, his "desertion"; it was not a shooting but an event to follow, a way back to possible safety. It happened. Responsibility was not an issue. Right or wrong was not an issue. How could it be?

The letter. My hand shaking like an uncontrolled thing. I could blame the hand. I was not responsible. But I had to write it.

Dear Lady (I had no idea of her name)

I am a friend of your husband. My name is Benjamin Routledge. He saved my life. Now I am in hospital in England. I have some nasty stomach injuries and will never live a normal life again.

I hope that he is okay and maybe he has come home on leave. (I very much doubted this would be true. Getting back to England was difficult enough)

I hope you can find some peace. (I have no idea why I said this)

If you get the time and if he can manage it I would like to get a letter from you, well maybe him.

I remain, your humble servant.

Etc. (I had already said my name and hated signing it)

It seemed so short and pathetic. I didn't want to tell her about the incident in the trench. Somehow it seemed distant and unimportant. Life was important, not pain and near death.

I went to bed sweating about the letter. Would it get there? Jamaica. The nurse promised. She smiled. I knew what was on her mind. I didn't mind that, but I suppressed those thoughts. Although my hand was at work more desperately that night. Nothing was forthcoming. Nothing gave me hope except for the idea of a letter or letters from strangers, written to me as a person.

I was a person, not just a number.

Chapter 7

I Open a Book
✳ ✳ ✳

The library drew me for other reasons. Books stood in file, soldiers undisturbed.

I wanted to find Cello's poem. "I am the captain of my soul." The last line was familiar, but what about the first? How could I find it?

"*MODERN ENGLISH POETRY*". How modern was modern? "*THE ROMANTIC POETS*". I was furtive in my search. I would be bullied without end if other patients caught me reading poetry ... of all things.

THE NINETEENTH-CENTURY POETS. THE OXFORD BOOK OF ENGLISH VERSE.

That was about it for poetry books, and none invited attention by their title or their appearance—dry and dusty, brown, with unturned pages, unopened covers. I was going to open them. But then my arm was like stone again. Fear of the unknown perhaps. Or fear of getting back to Cello, before his death ... execution. I wanted to move forward from that.

I sat down. I was so thin and gaunt. I walked like an old man. I didn't stick my chest out as with the pride of a soldier. There was no pride anymore. Anyway, I wanted to hide my "shit bag". So I would never stick out my chest and abdomen again. Folds of clothes would hide it from now on. I would bend at the waist. There was always pain anyway.

I had to go back to move forward. I had to know things and answer things in my head before going to see Cello's parents. I would need to be a rock against their grief.

I had no idea then how much I would need to be much more than a rock, which is a lifeless thing. I would have to be a life. But with my pale, stone clumsy hands and fingers like those of the dying, and a bag on my waist always full of shit (not piss, as that function I was still able to perform), I didn't have a feeling of life. I wanted to smoke, but a sign by the door forbade it because of the fire hazard.

I went out into the corridor and smoked with trembling hands. There was a chilly wind, and the end of my nose felt cold as I put the fag in and out of my mouth, smoking nervously. What was I? I caught a glimpse of myself in the window of the library, made like a mirror by the backing of books. Still, it was an impression, not a full image. I was gaunt, my body bent like a question mark where once I had been gay and straight and full of bravado. My uniform tunic was undone. I refused to do it up. My nose looked large as my face had fallen in somewhat.

Poetry—what an idiotic notion. But He drew me back, my "friend" Cello. Some things he did were so full of confidence, not a confidence borne of bravado but a genuine confidence of curiosity. I threw the fag butt, trod it dead, and went back into the library.

The books were within reach. I didn't need a ladder to get to books near the ceiling. This wasn't the British Library. I went for the *Oxford Book of English Verse*. It was a dark blue book with crocodile leather stem and edging and corners to its covers. The paper covering was mottled blue, with small patches of darker blue like blotting paper. Inside the front cover, the blotting paper continued, but this time there were more colours, including red and faint pink. I had of course seen books like this before, usually at school. There was something foreboding about them. Boys avoided them.

It was heavy and dense with the edges of the pages having the same mottled appearance but this time in a golden gilt sheen. In some respects, it seemed too beautiful to open. I had never thought of this sort of book as having a beauty of its own. But now I held it like a treasure, afraid to open it fully.

But then a surprise awaited me as I turned over the cardboard cover to a thick beige paper. Most of the books in the hospital library had been donated. They had not been bought new. This one was second hand and in the top left corner of the first inside facing page was a piece of handwriting, presumably from its original owner.

"Presented to Walter, by Walter (though paid for by his mother) in the hope that Walter."

Then nothing. I turned over the page to another pair of beige pages, which were completely blank. There was no continuation of this strange piece of handwriting. It appeared that Walter had got bored in the act of indicating what the book had been presented for, by himself. This was not a good omen, I thought. There were more blank pages, a title page, and then another with the words, "Chosen and edited by A. T. Quiller-Couch." At the bottom of the page: "Oxford at the Clarendon Press 1900." Over the page again was a strange address: *TO THE PRESIDENT FELLOWS AND SCHOLARS OF TRINITY COLLEGE OXFORD A HOUSE OF LEARNING ANCIENT LIBERAL HUMANE AND MY MOST KINDLY NURSE."*

What did all this mean? I was rapidly getting bored myself and had the feeling I was intruding into a world I had no place in. There was a PREFACE, which, while flipping through, I noticed some Greek writing. At least I assumed it was Greek.

Then I came to the first poem, which was entitled "Cuckoo Song." The English was obviously old-fashioned, as I could not even begin to understand it except for the words "Sumer and sing". I thought that was the wrong spelling of summer. It was dated on the right, c. 1250.

By now impatient, I randomly opened deep into the book and looked at the bottom of the lefthand page.

> My master and the neighbours all
> Make game of me and Sally
> And, but for her, I'd better be
> A slave and row a galley;
> But when my seven long years are out,
> O, then I'll marry Sally;
> O, then we'll wed, and then we'll bed-
> But not in our alley!

This seemed to me rather rubbishy and not fit for Oxford University, although that place was so far removed from my being that I would never have contemplated what would be fit for Oxford University.

Suddenly a visual memory came back to mind. After they shot Cello, I was wandering about and heard a truckful of officers singing a song about women and wine. They were singing in officers' accents with gusto, but the words were … well, I couldn't remember them, but they weren't memorable. They were probably like this and those; the officers, would have come from places like Oxford University. But as I read the verse again I realised that this wasn't like that. Officers would never live in an alley. That word was out of place. And "My master"? Officers do not have masters. They are the masters. A wave of disgust swept over me. They thought they were masters. In reality, they were masters of nothing!

With trembling hands, partly because of the chill and desolation in the room, I looked for some sort of index. I found the index of first lines.

My excitement grew. I never doubted that I would find Cello's poem. "Out of the night that covers me." But it did give me a thrill of discovery when I saw it. The number next to it was 842. Quickly I looked for that page. Lord Tennyson. "Unwatched the garden bough shall sway." Cello's poem was nowhere on this page. Back I went to the index, back to the page, then flicking through some other pages I noticed that the poems began with a number. IDIOT. It was the number of the poem.

Finally, I discovered it.

WILLIAM ERNEST HENLEY
Invictus.
Out of the night that covers me,
Black as the pit from pole to pole,
I thank whatever gods may be
For my unconquerable soul.
In the fell clutch of Circumstance
I have not winced nor cried aloud.
Under the bludgeonings of chance
My head is bloody but unbowed.
Beyond this place of wrath and tears
Looms but the horror of the shade,
And yet the menace of the years
Finds, and shall find me, unafraid.
It matters not how straight the gate,
How charged with punishments the scroll,

I am the master of my fate:
I am the captain of my soul.

I read it, then again and again, fast then slowly. I was afraid to read it aloud in case someone was watching and listening behind the half-closed door. But I made my lips move as I read it silently, as if I were speaking the words. I didn't want to put it down.

I was shaking, but not with cold. I could go back to bed if I had been cold, but I felt I could never go to bed again, at least not to seek rest there. My spirit could not rest again.

On the other hand, there was a sort of restful satisfaction in finding the poem. Poetry was a subject put aside after school. Who needed it in life? What did it mean? Some lines seemed nonsensical, but they left a feeling behind. They created an atmosphere in the air. They recreated Cello, his trial and punishment and finally the feeling that his end was not his end, at least not the end of his soul. Those words! No one needed them, as words, under ordinary circumstances. Perhaps for a wedding or a funeral, nothing else. Both of these would be in the hands of priests. But this and the title "Invictus". What did that mean?

I did not intend to become a priest, although we patients had discussed this as a way to get out of going back to the front. Then someone pointed out that there were lots of priests in the trenches. But actually most of those were Catholic ones, so become a priest of any other religion, and you would be safe.

Besides, they don't carry weapons, do they?

Back to thoughts of Cello again. His throwing away his rifle, a shocking crime for a soldier. Yet he made it seem the obvious thing to do. Stopping the war was simple—put down your weapons. Winning or losing, what did it matter anymore? There was no shame for him. In fact, he grew in stature without it. He grew in confidence and belief.

I was shaking still, but it was partly with an internal excitement. But now I did turn for bed, holding somewhere a sort of secret, a strange thing that was not explainable.

"What you been doing, Ben?" came the searching question from one little Nosey Parker.

"Oh, writing home, mate."

"Again, how come you suddenly start writing. You got a girl on tap, ain't ya? Where she from? How you meet 'er? Or is it a nurse? You're a crafty one. Quiet ones allay the worst. That was what my mammy used to say. Corse, I wasn't quiet."

"So you was … loud, were you, certainly loud enough now," commented another victim.

"That's enough from you. Don get off the subject. We want to know about Ben, don we, men?"

Then he started singing in a high tone music hall mimic:

> Ben, Ben tell us all then, whose your lady friend
> Hello, hello, who's your lady friend?
> Who's the little girlie beside your side?
> I've seen you, with a girl or two
> Oh oh-oh I am surprised at you
> Hello, hello, stop your little games
> Don't you think your ways
> You ought to mend?
> It isn't the girl
> I saw you with at Brighton
> Who, who
> Who's your lady friend?

During the song, which he knew word perfect, he rose up in bed, head craned forward, muscles straining, voice getting higher, finger wagging at me. Halfway through, others joined in, humming or mouthing along and finger-wagging as well.

The noise brought a nurse. I sank back, trying to laugh.

"He's got a girlfriend, nurse."

"No, I haven't." I managed a sort of snort instead of a laugh, and I felt cheated. My secret was sort of worthless. Whatever poetry I had found was different and meaningless here. My heart became heavy again. But the others were encouraged and started talking about a dance. There would be nurses, and they would surely have friends in the town. Woolwich boasted one of the country's biggest armaments factories. They waited until one of the young, vaguely pretty nurses, one without a matronly temperament, was on duty, and then they started working on her.

Suspicions as to me were forgotten. I was the outcast.

But the dance idea was eventually forgotten as well. We were patients, not partygoers. We had an unchanging place in the world, and we dropped back into it without a fight, some stepping further along the road to death.

My light of hope flickered perilously. My days of pain continued.

Chapter 8

On Receiving a Letter and Cleaning a Toilet
✳ ✳ ✳

Mail was brought to the wards by the senior duty day nurse. It made men happy, and so it must have been a pleasurable duty, unlike many.

Some men received letters and some didn't. Faithful wives and girlfriends who wrote often didn't necessarily make their men happy. Probably because they delivered their own cares and worries in the letters to men who could do nothing about them. The best ones were from girlfriends just met, through a hospital pen-pal scheme. The letters were hopeful of some future from well-meaning women. But the hope would soon wear off, especially when the pen-pals realised that the letters were being shared around a ward whose occupants held little hope of release unless on a one-way ticket back to a trench.

I was waiting every day, intensely expectant, though trying not to show it. I was one of those who did not generally receive letters. So it was not surprising that my letter was sort of sticking to a pile of those for one man who got a letter a day. He didn't always open them, just left them lying on his little bedside cupboard, with cigarettes and his personal ashtray.

A nurse almost threw them out. "Finished with these, have you? Oh, look, there's a couple you haven't opened. Hold on, this one's not even for you."

She read the envelope then looked across the ward. "It's for you, Private Routledge!"

I was stung by surprise and almost leapt up. She spun it across at me. Eyes followed. "Uuh, er, got a letter 'ave we Mr Routledge. The girlfriend, is it? *Who, who, who's your lady friend?*"

I tried to ignore them.

It was a small envelope which was probably why it nearly got missed. The address was in strange careful handwriting. Seeing my name gave a little rush of pleasure. It showed I had an independent life. I was nervous and opened it carefully I was not afraid.

The address was printed and not handwritten, this made it seem businesslike or perhaps just posh.

Hartwell
Coley Avenue
Reading

Dear Mr Routledge,

Your letter has made us so happy, but of course sad as well.

When we got the telegram from the War Office to say that Marcus had died in "the theatre of war", we could not understand the terminology and waited for some confirmation, daring to think perhaps, well, perhaps it had been a mistake.

But of course, the Army does not make mistakes like this, do they? But we needed confirmation, and now you have given it to us. We thank you for that most sincerely.

In the absence of any letter from Marcus's superiors, we are now looking to you to fill in so many gaps in our knowledge. The two things uppermost in our thoughts are, firstly, how did he die, or presumably get killed? Dying in "the theatre of war" seems a strange way of putting it and gives us no clues whatever. Secondly, we presume that he is buried in a temporary resting place. We understand from enquires that this is the normal practice and in time there might be a re-interment. This might not happen until after the war, but to know the whereabouts of his current resting place would be a comfort to us. Also, we really are interested to know where his cello is. As you know, it was his life. He was destined to be a good, possibly a great cellist. They are rare, so his cello remains important to us.

We realise that you are injured, and we wish you all the very best for a speedy recovery. We hope to meet you very soon. Please do take care of yourself and get stronger so that you can have a good future. We hope the war will be over soon with an end to this pointless slaughter, allowing all the boys to come home. The country and many families like ours have paid a far too high price already.

With every kind thought and wishing you good health. We look forward to hearing from you very shortly again.

Yours in hope,

Robert and Felicity Harris

It took me a long time to read the close and carefully written words. My eyes were wet as I finished it. The paper was thick. It was parchment. I had a stupid notion that I was holding a slice of bread, not a letter. A slice of bread was something that you did not drop or put aside lightly. You looked for a clean and pure place to put it before buttering and eating it.

In the trenches, we did sometimes have bread and butter. You nursed it carefully before sitting in a selected place and eating it with slow and singleminded pleasure. Once Jack and I both dropped ours in a pool of filthy mud water. We were drunk and just laughed and swigged more rum.

It was a moment of shared brotherhood. But the possibility of those moments in the future, either eating fresh bread or drinking rum slipped away as cello came back to me in this letter. Further, I realised that whereas before I was subject to the army for everything and despite everything I had maintained an agreement to that, a sort of contract that let me be led by an unwritten loyalty. Now that had broken suddenly. Some ideas were now above all that.

I needed time to understand what was in the letter and what it meant to me. I knew there was some terrible truth there that would make me face in an even more bitter way the events of Cello's death.

I put the letter aside unable to take it all in at once.

I also needed my health and strength. So I carefully folded the letter, put it back in the envelope, and placed it in the drawer of my bedside cabinet. I thought I would take a long time before facing it again.

I must have had a faraway look about me, as many men did when reading letters, so no one challenged me about it.

I took it out again as soon as the lights were turned down for sleep. I got out of bed and took my army coat from its peg behind the bed. I shuffled out of the ward in search of some light to read it by. Waking eyes would be watching, but they might take it as another trip to the library. Any re-reading or special attention to a letter was taken as a sign that you were breaking away from the brotherhood of depressing predictability that made up our lives, and that would be targeted for a special session of bullying.

Lights at night were hard to find in the hospital. They burned over nurses' desks. Our ward did not have a resident night nurse, as we were all regarded as stable, in a medical sense, at any rate. Our injuries did not burst in the night. No one was on the point of dying. We had no mental cases, at least not those who were documented as such.

The corridor had lights, dim ones, high in the ceilings and interspersed by yards of darkening road. Anyone lurking there would be swept up by patrols of senior nurses. I got into a toilet and closed the door. It would be the best place. With my bag around my waist, I spent quite a long time in the toilets doing messy things. So I had an excuse for the time.

I took out the letter, and my hands began to tremble.

"Saying Marcus had died in the theatre of war."

"You to fill in so many gaps in our knowledge."

Some phrases just lifted from normal life left me totally cold and alone. I had to clean up the mess of war. Everyone just closed their eyes and minds, leaving the battlefield littered with broken things, a broken world.

Once I had actually fully accepted that the War Office, or whoever it was that sent out the telegrams, had not actually communicated the fact that Cello had been court-martialled for desertion and executed, I realised that my loyalty and my faith in king and country was all for nothing. I was a number, a rifle, a rifleman. I was nothing, and neither was Cello.

Then in a moment, the whole story came back to me. The president of Cello's court-martial, on hearing that he was actually a real cello player, had gone mad. We, who were associated with the accused, had been led to believe by the military police that he was merely suffering from a heart attack and unable to continue. But we knew there was something deeper going on.

The president suddenly realised that the war was killing good people. Well, a classical musician was, in his eyes, a good person. Before soldiers were perhaps unthinking brutes, who could be thrown over the line in hordes, to stem the Boche. Regrettable, but It had to be done. But now, here in front of him was one of them who had a connection to his world.

What was his world? Well, he was posh? He was upper class. He loved classical music and no doubt attended concerts at the Albert Hall and whatever other halls were attended by such people. In front of him, as he settled back in his seat in his dinner suit and turned his attention to the ladies and gentlemen of the orchestra, he might have seen Cello playing his cello, playing Bach. The name suddenly sprang from my memory like a dart. That had been the word that had sent the president into a kind of trance—a German musician, composer. You might have thought he had suddenly seen another crime in the playing of German music. But no, this was higher than war, something untouched by such a mean thing as war. But now it had been touched. Its purity had been broken. So his madness was not about Cello himself but maybe about how the president's world had been suddenly broken.

Maybe things would be clearer now.

A smell filled the toilet. My bag was overfull. It worked like an intestine that should have been inside. It just filled up on its own, much to the disgust of people around you. I clamped the hose and removed the bag carefully. I sloshed the contents into the toilet. Then I suddenly froze physically, remembering that this toilet was out of bounds due to the flush not working. Why had they not locked it? I replaced the bag and then realised that the paper had been removed as well. Toilet paper was short and was strictly rationed.

I cared not for this dilemma. I did not care to be considerate anymore.

Putting the letter away and trying to conceal my bag back on my waist, I tried to leave. My luck was out; a night nurse was just leaving her duty at one of the wards and saw me. The night staff were disliked. They did not try to become acquainted with the patients as did the day nurses. Every activity was a disliked chore to them, except when they had to reprimand a patient for some misdemeanour. They enjoyed that.

"You know that toilet is out of bounds, don't you?"

"I have a bag. I was taken short needed to empty—"

"You do not get taken short with a bag. You have plenty of time to find another lavatory; BUCKET AND MOP, OVER THERE." She pointed to the cupboard some way along the corridor.

I had to mop my excrement from the lavatory and wash it down another one farther down the corridor, then clean everything. She stood aside as I did it, watching, arms folded, face screwed against the odour.

"BLEACH PLEASE."

I disinfected everything. I wasn't allowed to disinfect myself by bathing. It was not bath time.

I decided I would get out of that hospital. I would see Cello's parents and tell them everything. I would need every bit of courage I didn't think I possessed, but I would do it.

Chapter 9

The Handwriting of an Angel
✳ ✳ ✳

I now knew for certain that I was lucky, because I understood what would make me get better—hope. Whatever medical things happened if I clung onto a fragment of hope I could survive and get out of the hospital and live, something of a life. If one road to hope came to a dead end, I could replace it with another. If one letter did not receive a reply, I would write another that might.

But in the case of my first two letters, they both received replies.

The reply from Midnight's wife gave me both anguish and guilty excitement in equal measure.

Dear Mister Routledge,

Your letter came as a joy to me. I don't know whether you are a religious man, but God always lifts you up when you are laid low by grief. Belief in him brings rewards. Your letter was my reward from him. The grief was caused by the loss of my beloved husband Damien (I did not know Midnight's real name).

I was informed of his death only last week. I am raw with grief. He was my heart and soul and my future. It seemed that the future is very dark now, but then I received your letter. You said he saved your life. How good that makes my heart feel. I know he was a good man and now I know his life was not in vain. He was meant to save you perhaps.

You wished me peace. Perhaps deep down you knew he would get killed. Well I can tell you that your letter has brought me peace, in great measure.

But forgive my selfishness I have not spared a thought or word for you and your injury. I am sure it is terrible. But now I have the chance to wish you peace and god speed in your recovery. I hope that you will often write to me.

With all kind thoughts,

Joyce Pearl JOHNSTON

The letter, beautifully handwritten, included a very small photo of her. Midnight's death seemed tragic, but in a strange guilty way, it seemed destined to happen.

I was numb and trembling, and tears streamed down my face. I could not hold the photo. I dropped it and then picked it up dusty from the library floor where I had retreated to read the letter. Rare early winter sunlight streamed through the high windows of the library making tunnels of light. I brought the photo into one of them, my blanketed body hunching to examine it better. I could not imagine a lovelier face. It smiled at me with bright teeth. The eyes danced a bit, and dark hair hung over them temptingly. The dress was patterned in simple squares. I thought it was like a beauty queen's dress, but actually, it was more like a sort of Sunday school one. I could not fathom that moment. It gripped me so greatly. I hunched and rocked and cried silently. I felt so unclean against the obvious purity of this woman, whose mystery filled me with such excitement that I knew I would become ill.

So it was. My body could not heal completely. It would never do that. I was constantly susceptible to infection and stomach problems. Then, of course, externally I was this horrible hunched figure, the shadow of my former straightness, with a smelly grey bag of shit permanently attached to my waist with a pipe going into my stomach. In the trenches, these areas of our bodies were sources of constant jokes and investigation. Now it was the source of dread, pain, and embarrassment, especially when thinking of relations with women. My stomach problems and my physical state also led to fevers, which my body was not well equipped to fight. My actual entry wound was still not fully healed. Sometimes the whole thing became infected with sores that wept puss.

I had to stay in bed for days, and my fever increased. The others watched me in fascination. Should I die, they would try to get something from my things. There was not much to get.

But I was not going to die, at least not before I did certain things.

What were those things?

Some of them were obvious in my mind. I had to see Cello's parents. There lay a kind of dread. They didn't know he had been executed. They hadn't got his cello back. This was my opportunity, to tell the truth, to finally set right the wrong done to him. It was me that had to do it. But if I could get the cello back first and go there with a present, perhaps they would forgive me!

To help me I had someone in the background who had already taken up a place in my heart. But I knew where my heart was in my body and feelings of the heart came as a sort of pain in that area that often slipped into the stomach and got translated into rumblings of nerves and digestive juices, which in my case ended in disgust. But Cello was in my soul. I could not identify that area of my body. To some, it was nowhere. To me, it had become everywhere.

In my fever, I thought I had lost Midnight's wife's letter. I was suddenly in despair. I should write straight away to her. Then I got into a panic, filled with guilt about my thoughts, and I considered that I needed to put her aside and concentrate on Cello's parents' letter and the actions that loomed large from it.

I needed to write to them. I needed to see them. How would I get his cello back to them?

It all seemed impossible until coincidentally a strange release seemed to open to me and some of my fellow patients. A memo came to all patients about the possibility of leave. Perhaps we had reached our required sentence duration in this prison-like hospital. There was talk that the hospitals had become so full that they had to get some of the patients out on leave. Ours was a general hospital, but many had become specialists, we heard, dedicated to limbless men, neurological units, orthopaedic units, cardiac units, typhoid units, and venereal diseases. But the idea that some of the casualties who were recovering might be better off at home did not seem to occur to the authorities. Casualties were to be treated so that they could return to the front as quickly as possible. Or to ensure they were invalided out as fit as possible so that they wouldn't get a big pension.

It was a standing joke in the hospital that you had more leave when in the trenches than you got from the hospital. It was also often compared to being in a military prison.

I begged to be allowed to go on leave. The process was complicated; a request in writing, on Army Form QX5846, followed perhaps by a medical board, an interview, and then a wait. We didn't know how long that would be.

We celebrated Christmas waiting. This was a bizarre experience. We were the lucky ones but were more like the forgotten ones.

One was dressed up as Father Christmas. The red tablecloth that he ingeniously tied around himself reminded me of the one at Cello's court-martial. He used stuff that was plentiful in the hospital—safety pins (after cutting up the blanket to pin arms), cotton wool (for the beard, of course), bandages for various other things.

He came on us in the ward to applause, dragging a kitchen tray by a bandage tied around his waist. That was where the plentiful things ran out. A brown paper package for each of us hardly filled the tray. There were a few letters from home, cards, most of them. One for me from my parents asked me to "get well soon!" No personal message.

The "presents" were given out, just jokey things that we had drawn lots to present to each other. A pair of socks found in the corridor. A cigar, was a genuinely good present, which the man had received from his parents, gave us a rare moment of real pleasure as we passed it around.

I could see the man in the opposite bed crying, openly, which was unusual, as emotions normally needed to be buried to cut down the bullying. Sampson might be dying. I had had so little time for my fellow patients. But now this loneliness brought us together and suddenly Sampson, the strong one, usually a trickster and a bit of a bully himself, was dying.

They baked a Christmas cake for us in the kitchen, and the staff nurses came and shared it with us. Some even sat on our beds. I think we were all crying by then.

It was a shared loneliness, not made easier for that. There were no visitors.

The day drew to a close. It must have been the strangest Christmas any of us had spent. We were supposed to be the lucky ones, who had made it back alive, just, even not really very badly injured, as most of my present ward had miscellaneous injuries. Two or three stomach ones like mine. Another had lost the lower part of his face, but as he hadn't lost a limb, they couldn't categorise him as a "limbless casualty". He was quite fit bodily and therefore would be difficult for the medical board to categorise. They had covered what remained of the face with skin and constructed a kind of new mouth and nose for him, but they couldn't send him out into the world with them. The new face was too horrific to behold. So he was destined to spend his life in institutions. All of us wanted to break out, but we were held back. We blamed the army, but perhaps we were ourselves afraid.

"Are we having a New Year's Eve dance then?" someone said as the evening wore on and loneliness finally silenced us. There were all the ingredients, nice nurses and time and even music over a scratchy tannoy sometimes. But we knew there would be no dance.

I determined to return to the library on the next day.

I picked up the *Oxford Book of English Verse* again, seeking something outside my loneliness. I just opened it.

The name WILLIAM WORDSWORTH headed the page.

My eyes were drawn immediately to an indented set of four lines near the top of the facing page:

> O Joy! that in our embers
> Is something that doth live,
> That nature yet remembers
> What was so fugitive!

I read it again and again, then continued on down the page, not really understanding but revelling strangely, the words, about nature and spring (*Feel the gladness of the May*) that was so distant from this place.

Then I focussed on four lines with margins muddled strangely.

> Though nothing can bring back the hour
> Of splendour in the grass, of glory in the flower:

> We will grieve not, rather find
> Strength in what remains behind;

This was enough. It was not more than Cello's poem, found by himself and brought to us and to his execution as a sort of victory over his last moments. But this was my own find, not as a comforter for my last moments but as a path to shape my future.

It was a kind of hope, more than a mother's gloved hand. It was a secret scroll delivered into my hand, to do with as I needed.

In those few moments, my frail spine, bent as it was, seemed to draw upon something. My thoughts went to some bizarre fact dredged from my memory. I had got some more straw for my bricks.

I got up and replaced the book, not before I placed a fragment of brown paper torn surreptitiously from that which was peeling away from the wall in the far bottom corner of the room, into the book, to mark the page.

I went back to the ward and found on my bed a form authorising my leave for two weeks' time.

Chapter 10

A Journey via a Pub
✳ ✳ ✳

I wrote to Cello's parents telling them that I had been granted some leave and would now like to come and see them. Almost immediately I received a reply to say that they would be willing to greet me on any day and at any time and that I could stay at their house for some days. *Our dear son's room is free for you.*

I knew I had to go there without the cello. Getting it back would be a virtually impossible task. Like the dead Cello and now the dead Midnight, who could not be brought back to life, the cello was a dead thing.

How wrong this thought would turn out to be.

I had not left the hospital, except to walk gingerly in the gardens before the cold set in. Army uniform and coat hardly kept out the rawness of the day I left the hospital. My skin felt thin and vulnerable. For January it was not as bad as it could have been. I held a small canvas suitcase, which held some clean underwear and a shirt. I waited on the pavement for a tram, which eventually took me down the hill towards Woolwich, its engine moaning as though it were climbing up a steep hill.

My fellow passengers eyed me, women mostly, in dark, greasy raincoats with headscarves. They were going to the munitions factory in the Royal Arsenal. A faint odour emanated from them. I recognised it as an explosive powder. We passed barracks. Woolwich was a military town. Parade grounds were there, and I saw squads marching, but few soldiers seemed to be travelling into town. Those on the tram as I got on, outside the hospital, would know I was a casualty. They could not see any visible signs of that, so they would possibly put a nasty label on me, shirker or something like that. I could see that in their eyes.

"Where to, sir?" Asked the conductor, with a very slight pause before the "sir", as he could see I was not an officer.

"The railway station."

"Yeah, which one, mate? We got two of 'em." He had quickly decided that I wasn't worth a sir.

"Well, I don know."

"It's on yur pass. You got yur pass?" Now he was suspicious. Every soldier in uniform had to have a pass and, if he was travelling, a rail warrant. I managed to fish it out of my coat.

"Oh, Woolwich … Dockyard."

"Well, they gave you a duff one there mate. Should've given it to you from the Arsenal. That's where we'll end up. Then you gotta bit of a walk, down Powis street, up into Parson's Hill, across to St Mary's Street, then you'll eventually get to Station Road.

"Oh, well, will you tell me when to get off?"

"Don't worry, mate. Everyone gets off at the Arsenal. Can't exactly miss it."

I gave him one of the slips of a ticket designated for interstation travel.

The women two seats away were giggling by this stage.

I sat back, feeling exhausted already, and uncomfortable, as this was the first time I had been out in public with my bag.

We passed down the hill, which swept towards the River Thames. At the bottom was a great market area. People milled and crossed around everywhere, constantly passing in front of the tram. There were men in suits and hats, shopping women not destined for the munitions factory, stall-keepers wearing stripped aprons, and boaters on the verges of their canopies that stretched out from shop fronts.

The station was below street level. Steam and smoke wafted up, like a smoke signal, giving away the location. As I got down the noise of a train came as a mournful hoot, like a demented giant owl. It annoyed me, because I knew it heralded a departure for those returning from leave to the front or new recruits leaving for the first time, perhaps from the Artists Rifles. But I was directed away from the station. I felt stupid, having to walk to another one. Powis Street was long and straight, with high shop fronts. Its bustle gradually diminished as I walked away from the central part of the town.

I came to the end and on the corner with Parsons Hill was a public house called the Castle Tavern. I needed a rest from carrying my case. Freedom and the smell of beer, spirit, and stale tobacco attracted me. I needed to smoke anyway. I could do it in comfort with a nip of something. The pub seemed to have different doors, and I chose the "lounge bar". Inside were several bench seats against a bare smoke-stained wall. The barmaid was large, wearing a dirty apron and a scarf knotted at the front of her head. Delivery lorries whined their way up and down the street outside. Horses hooves rang on cobbles, and their carts squeaked and bumped like the horsedrawn ammo carts that plied the mud roads up to and from the front line. Unlike those, delivery boys called out their wares. I closed the door to shut out thoughts of France.

"What can I get you, mister?" I looked at the shelves behind where dusty bottles resided. I searched for rum instinctively. I tore my eyes away. I was not used to drinking, and rum would make me feel tipsy. I had a long journey ahead and had hardly started yet.

My eye was drawn to an advert painted along the edge of the shelf that held the spirit bottles. "Meux's Original London Stout, 6p a nip. DRAWN FROM THE WOOD. India Pale Ale, per glass 4p—6p per half a pint." I started and looked again. The prices looked as though they had been scrubbed out and repainted.

The barmaid was waiting impatiently. "A shilling a pint," I said. "Since when?"

"Since that bastard in number ten, who's a teetotaller, decided to raise the duty." The voice came from behind me. I turned and reviewed the speaker, who sat smoking in the corner of one of the bench seats. He was holding a pint in the free hand. He wore a black hat and suit that seemed frayed everywhere. As I looked, he tipped his hat. "But let me buy you one. Look as though you could use it. On leave, are we? Joyce, give the lad a pint, would you?"

The barmaid immediately started drawing on a wooden pump, then plumped the glass full of cloudy brown ale, with a small layer of cream bubbles on top, handle towards me, on the bar.

"Yes, just going on leave," I said.

"Saucy Worcesters, eh?" he announced.

"Eh?"

"Worcestershire Regiment." He had seen my cap badge.

"You know of these things," I admitted.

"I know a bit ... an I must say, I 'ope you got yer morale back, coz they shot some of yur regiment for cowards, din they. Five was it, from the same regiment. My, that's going some."

I was suddenly struck as though by a rock, not a bullet in the face. It punched rather than pierced, and my face must have sprung up like a red tomato. "Well I, well I can't ..."

"No no, can't talk about those things, can we? 'Ours not to reason why is it ... some thins happen in war, don they' ... But you're a bit far from home, ain't yer? Where you going on leave?"

He mercifully changed the subject. "Reading."

He nodded as I raised my glass in thanks then he cocked his head thoughtfully to one side. "So why didn't yer go from the Arsenal dirict? Seems you goin bit of a roundabout route, eh?"

"Yeah, they gave me a warrant from the Dockyard station, not Arsenal."

"Shouldn't 'ave done that. Seems funny."

I knew what he was after. I knew he was suspicious. He would probably know what regiments were in the barracks, and I was trying to pass myself off as coming straight from France. Maybe I could say I was on a course in the barracks here. Yes, that was it. But I just drank my beer nodding. I had not planned or thought of this situation at all.

After a long pause, the inevitable question came. "You from the hospital, are yer?"

I began to sweat immediately, and I also needed the lavatory. I had been stupid to think I could pass off for anything else. Men from France carried their equipment and rifle with them. Many of them still had mud on their boots. But I was clean and probably smelt of hospital. Yes, that was it. I couldn't get away from it. "Well ... I ... yes, I am."

"Thought as much." He threw his head up in a kind of triumph at his powers of observation. Then he drew himself in and quaffed his beer off quickly, as if he didn't want to drink with me.

Aware of the very few bits of change in my pocket I quickly offered him a drink. "Can I buy you a half don't have much money, I'm afraid."

"No, lad. Hang onto yur money. Yur gonna need it."

I left the place with a terrible taste in my mouth, not just from the beer. The news he had given me made it almost impossible to walk. I felt so heavy, whereas when I left the hospital, I had felt a lightness, as if everything had been lifted from me. Now everything was back with a vengeance. I didn't know whether he had spoken of Cello, whether he knew about Cello.

The regiment had had a very difficult time since arriving in France in 1914. We had heard of things in other battalions. But most of the time you lived by the minute, not interested in the next trench.

It was an easyish walk to the station after that. Once there, I felt in better hands. Trains were well organised, regular, and a military precision was in place, regulated by the paper I had with me. I was not known and not therefore questioned. It was down on the warrant, and I could depend on that. I needed a little money for food. The train had toilets, and I could withdraw into myself.

London's mainline Waterloo station came upon us. Station staff shouted directions above the banging of doors. "Paddington Station. Everyone for Paddington, down the stairs, follow the signs, take the next train … the next train." We shuffled along. Few had become many, most in uniform or suits. No one eyed me like the man in the pub. No one questioned.

On reaching Paddington came another change. "Reading, please?"

"Reg'lar service there, platform number one." He stamped my warrant.

Staff was in abundance, so you could always ask. Soot penetrated my mouth, hoots were in my ears, smoke swirled around the platform. Every soldier was used to the train as troop trains took everyone to the front. This was not a goodbye and a journey to terror. This was a kind of adventure, and I was thankful for it. But I was going to a place for which my emotions were totally untrained and unready. I suppose Reading was not a place to be unready in.

The journey was uneventful. I had no room to myself, except the space of my seat. I sat next to the door and could not lose myself in the passing countryside. I worried that I smelt of the usual contents of my bag, but the other smells, of tobacco, the train, and other people, were strong enough to mask it, I suppose. There was the bustle of people up and down the corridor and the occasional visit by the guard asking for "all tickets please."

That gave the opportunity for passengers to view each other. The window gazers turned and produced their tickets with a tut tut. Or at least those who saw themselves as posh did. That was one couple sitting near the window on the far side. Others produced their tickets meekly.

The war made travellers of us all, levelling the class barriers a little. But there was still a separation between first, second, and third class on the trains. Those in the front line could only travel when released. But leave did create a wonderful release from the shackles of the trenches, and men spoke of strange and mysterious meetings while on their journeys home. On arrival though a kind of heavy expectation set in, and within a couple of days the dread of return began to creep into your bedroom with you. Return was never far away. The army's grip never loosened.

I had only been on leave once and hadn't enjoyed it.

This was different, and I thought it might have an element of adventure about it. I even began to get a bit of my old spirit back, the one I lost when Cello was shot, a cynical spirit.

A group of soldiers were drinking and smoking in the corridor. Their laughter was infectious, and I smelt rum. I caught sight of them, but they weren't close enough for eyes to meet. But I did want a rum.

I slept a bit and was jolted awake by doors banging. "Reading, READING!"

I jumped up. I didn't have much to collect, so I was able to leave the train before it moved on again.

"Oh, Coley Avenue, up with the posh nobs, eh!"

It was uphill and had to be a taxi ride as trams did not get there.

Chapter 11

I Say Three Small Words
✳ ✳ ✳

I had not had an upbringing filled with childish emotions. A touch on the arm or downward glance together with a wave of my father's hand—"Off you go then, lad"—was supposed to be an expression of a parent's regard and care for their son. In reality, it was an interruption to prevent things getting too close to an emotion that might answer a question of life, such as, "Why are the relatives shouting at us?"

Relatives were a rare appearance at our home and always came at a time of some family calamity that caused the shouting. An aunt dying suddenly of TB was one I remembered, although I never knew the aunt and didn't attend the funeral. A drunken brawl with someone who I had called uncle before, had brought blood to the stone floor of the hall.

There were silences for days after these incidents. I had no brothers or sisters to confide in or fight with. That would have been better than the silence.

I was therefore not at all prepared or ready for what I found in Cello's home. A house set back from the tree-lined avenue.

"Let us settle you down in your room Benjamin then we will wait for you in the drawing room." The mother was attentive to the very last detail. "These are new pyjamas." It was not my room, but I was not expected to wear Cello's actual clothes, especially his pyjamas. The new ones were folded at the bottom of the bed. I suddenly longed to put them on. The army did not provide such clothing. The hospital did, but some men had got theirs from home. Others wore long underwear. I had acquired a nightshirt from a patient who had died. I had not brought that with me.

"Just call down if you need anything." Then she stood for a moment, drinking me in with a sad half-smile before withdrawing and closing the door quietly.

I looked around, and it was as if I saw the silence. The room was oppressively silent. No sound reached me, and my life seemed to be standing still. It was a room … almost a room to die in. The walls had dark paper. The bed and furniture were dark brown. Curtains hung heavy and still and roped back. It was almost dark outside. I would need a light in the room soon, but there didn't seem to be one. Did the house have electricity, or were they using gas lamps? Through the window, bare January trees stood unmoved by my looking at them.

From my suitcase, I removed the *Oxford Book of English Verse*, which I had borrowed from the hospital library. Well, I hadn't actually borrowed it in the sense that you would normally borrow from a library with a librarian recording your book and stamping it with a return date. I had borrowed it without seeking permission to do so. But I was confident that the book would not be missed. I put it down by the bed on the little table. I lifted the heavy bed cover gingerly. Yes, the sheets were white. This was a bed I should have relished, together with the pyjamas. But there was a foreboding about the situation.

I could not put off my appearance in the drawing room any longer. I had nothing more to do. So I stepped out of the room into the equally dark corridor. Still no sound came to me. The stairs creaked, of course, which must have heralded my approach, for the mother came out of the drawing room to meet me. There was a low light in the room, which made me feel a little comforted. "Come on, Benjamin."

"Thank you." I stood.

"Please come and sit down, Benjamin." The father was seated in an armchair in front of a dying fire, and he indicated the one next to him. The mother settled herself on the settee. "Perhaps you would like a bottle of beer," said the father.

"No, thank you. I did have a drink on the train." I sat down.

"We usually have a drink of tea before bed," said the mother. "But food is scarce, you know."

"I'm so sorry ..." I blurted out as if it were Cello I was talking to. It was what I should have said to him.

"Benjamin, it's not your fault." The mother twisted to the side, her long skirt arranged neatly, hands folded in her lap. She sat still as she said it, then remained expectantly poised. The father in a dark suit had his right hand on his face, stroking whiskers.

The single light in the room came from a small table lamp, which was electric. It enlarged the shadows of their faces as it came from low down.

I had not made up my mind about anything to say, a story. One suddenly formed itself in my voice. "I should have been there, but I didn't see exactly what happened. Something happened, and it led to a charge being framed against Cello."

They sat totally still. Nothing moved in the room. The father stopped stroking his whiskers, moved his hand slowly from his face, and then it dropped to his knee. With it, his head jerked a little upwards. "A CHARGE!" he spoke in his officer-like voice.

"Yes," I tumbled on. Suddenly I could believe anything I said. "He was charged with desertion and court-martialled ... and found guilty. Then, THEY SHOT HIM!"

In the trenches, death was often a joke, shrugged off to keep the bravado going, and I had momentarily reverted to my trench self.

There was a sudden strangled intake of breath from the mother as if indeed she had been shot.

Afterwards, I thought I could have said that I had killed him in the heat of battle and brought the blame onto myself that way. But seeking their forgiveness for that instead of the real crime would have been like doubling the crime and a pure deceit.

Now I had got rid of my guilt in a flash, transferring it to "them".

The father was totally motionless. Then after a moment, he stood straight up to attention, again like an officer. "Shot him! Do you mean his own soldiers?"

I nodded. I was in tears.

"I'm sorry. I have to leave you for a moment." Without a further word, he left the room.

Cello's mother turned her head as if it was hardly attached to her body.

"ROBERT!" she managed to cry out. Then she too stood and ran from the room.

I heard them in another room, moving about. Then suddenly a noise split the silent house like a cleaver. A high-pitched scream followed by a terrible deep-throated sob that dropped to the depths of the house and its deep brown furniture, as if the house itself was twisting and the wood splintering under a terrible force. Then an uncontrolled crying started and seemed to go on and on. It made me think of the crying of the casualty that we had heard in the trenches and that made us go out to find him, leading to everything that had brought me to this moment, a moment that seemed to be the breaking of every way of thinking of civilisation that had built up in my life.

Then a sharp slap broke the crying. My cheeks burned suddenly.

I had not been subjected to beating as a child, not by my parents, though at school the cane was a constant companion to the teacher and often wielded in front of the class. But that was the stuff of bravado and hero-making, not of shame.

How could Cello's parents now face me? I thought of the unsaid things in my parents' home, and I knew it would be the same here. Perhaps therein lay my escape.

But looking around I realised that there was no escape.

The crying had dropped to a low moan, like a strange wind. I sat gripping the arms of my chair and knowing that I would need to find the toilet soon. But I waited.

A noise outside the room made me sit up. The father entered. He stood a little hesitantly and his face beneath the whiskers appeared red and slightly distorted, as if he was endeavouring to keep his mouth closed. "Benjamin, we do appreciate all that you have done … we have much to discuss and try to find out. As for now, I think it is best we all sleep on it and meet again in the morning. Can you find your way to your room or—?"

"Yes, yes, but I need to use the lavatory. Where is it?"

"Follow me." He led me up the stairs and indicated a small room at the end of the upstairs corridor. It had a light.

After my sordid business in the lavatory, I crept out and listened for movement from below. The crying seemed to have ceased. I heard faint sounds of glass and then a single word: "DRINK."

I retreated to my room. I took off my uniform and carefully put on the pyjamas. The bed felt cold. I realised it was January and should have been colder. But the eiderdown on top of me felt heavy, so I knew that I would be warm enough. The warmth I quickly began to build up inside the bed did not match the atmosphere outside it. I listened for some clues as to the activity in the house but heard nothing.

The night brought terrible dreams. I had become used to these. Tunnels and trenches and forgetting my rifle featured in most of the dreams. Trying to rescue Cello was a regular feature. An impossible journey across deep ravines and mountains or holes full of mud and bodies brought me to a coffin in which there was only dust or a skeleton. I was often carrying a decaying body. It usually came apart in my arms.

Chapter 12

Hoping for a Terrible Mistake
✳ ✳ ✳

I woke during darkness. Hospital did not allow late sleeping. Morning medication and sisters' rounds demanded our presence. They tried to make it as though we were still in the army, which of course we were. Here I was on leave. I could sleep all day if I wanted. Not in this house.

A greyness was arriving outside the window. In the trenches, the dawn woke you. Inside you always missed it, depending which way your window was facing. My present window seemed shaded on the inside by the heavy curtains and on the outside by some overgrowth of ivy or wisteria. The sentinels in the garden still stood there.

I got up, bracing myself against the cold. This would probably improve my health, being out of the hospital. Thus the chances of me getting a clean bill of health and sent back to the front would increase. I still didn't know whether my condition would entitle me to a discharge.

I hesitated to leave my bedroom for fear of what I might discover in the house. I had brought tragedy, but what had been here before? Something made me fear the outside of my door as I had never feared my own home, for all its family tribulations. Yet how could Cello, who seemed to tower above me in spirit, have come from a house where fear resided?

I picked up the *Oxford Book of Verse* and started flipping through it. Then I threw it on the bed. What did these useless words give me. Only Cello's example gave me something.

Having put on Cello's spirit like his dressing gown, I decided to make brave.

Daily washing for troops was a discipline that could be escaped only during sustained operations. Afterwards, and especially when coming out of the line, washing and shaving were mandatory. In some battalions, discipline for such things and the cutting of hair slipped, but only until a general officer arrived to inspect. After that, a battalion commander might be replaced. It made little difference to us. Only the company commanders, who were more experienced and less tired than the platoon commanders, made a difference by their presence and character.

But discipline usually filtered down through the senior NCOs, and shaving had been drummed into us. So I crept to the bathroom and surveyed the plumbing. Not every house had running water. This one did. I took out my safety razor and went to work listening for sounds in the house. These razors were a small luxury given to us by the hospital. Cut throats were too dangerous for men with terrible injuries, particularly mental ones. A man could easily cut his own throat accidentally or deliberately.

I did not hear anything other than the water. The noise of my washing and shaving must have woken the whole neighbourhood—such was the gurgling and sucking from the pipes.

Afterwards bringing my braces back up, I returned to the room, with Cello's dressing gown.

Finally fully dressed, I purposely made a noise leaving my room. The stairs creaked, and suddenly I became aware of Cello's mother standing at the end of the corridor around the corner of the stairs. It must have been the door to the kitchen, where I had heard them the night before. She stood like a ghost, very still, arms by her side, as though she had been there all night. She wore a long skirt, possibly the same as the night before, and a high-collared white blouse. "Robert's gone to work," she said simply.

"I didn't know he … what does he …?" It was a relief to talk in what seemed normal voices. But I was used to this ignoring, brushing under the carpet, of what had gone before in conversations.

"He works in munitions supply, civilian side. I don't have a job, d'you see. I am … was a musician. I helped Marcus with his practice. Of course, he was way ahead of me. But I teach a little … now."

"That's nice," I said uselessly.

"Yes. Would you like some breakfast. We don't have much, perhaps porridge and bread, though it will be very thinly sliced, and tea."

"That would be very nice Mrs … Harris."

"You can sit at the table. I will bring it." She indicated a dining room, which was small, but on entering, I was struck suddenly by the photographs on the sideboard. There was Cello with his instrument, his mother beside him, and on the floor a trophy. He must have been about seventeen years old. Then I noticed another one, to the side. Cello was young, perhaps ten yours old, dressed in an immaculate sailor suit. His mother was seated on a bench. Standing on the bench was another boy, fair and a little chubby, but with clear similarity in looks. There was no other sign of the brother in the house.

The breakfast arrived, a very small bowl of porridge, bread like cardboard with an invisibly tiny smudge of butter on it and a cup of tea, which did have a mixture of milk.

"I see Cello has a brother," I blurted out, my need to make conversation continuing.

She put the tray down slowly. "Did have …"

"Oh." I knew straight away I could not take that further. It remained in the air. She sat down very carefully. She was like a musical instrument in the way she moved, although no sound came from her body. Her face was a mask set like a waxwork piece of art.

I waited for her to say something as I could eat without the need for conversation. Any further words of mine would probably cause more damage.

Eventually she did speak. "Of course we have no information as to what you imparted last night. My … husband will take this up with the army authorities. "Then her voice broke somewhat. "There must surely be … some mistake. Of course, it must have been very terrible for you, but … but, mistake, do you … ?"

Suddenly I felt a power, the power of information. "I saw him shot. There was no mistake about that. But MISTAKE, yes, the whole episode was a mistake. It should never have happened."

My words, born of my relaxation in speaking, made her shudder. "'I saw him shot,'" brought her to reality with a jolt. But then she seemed elated if that could be possible, rushing away from the reality. She was clutching for something, and I had given it to her. "Yes, YES. We both knew it. It was a mistake." She clasped her hands together.

I had my escape. The confusion of battle had created the mistake. I didn't know what happened. But then suddenly she turned back to me in earnest. "You saw him ... when they?"

"Yes, I'm sorry, but he asked me to be there for him." Now I could tell the truth. It seemed brutal and terrible to speak about an execution with a certain ... joy. But we were exploring the truth.

"I knew it. You were his real friend. He never mentioned any friends, but we knew he must have had some ... one at least." Her voice trailed off into nothing. She was still waiting. "And the shooting, was it ...?" She seemed to be convincing herself that he had been in a kind of battle, with the firing squad as the enemy.

"It was brave. He died so bravely. You sent him his cello, and he was overjoyed. He even got ... I'm sorry but I have to say this, his firing squad, to sing a song, and he played to it."

She almost leapt in a half-laugh, but actually, it was a scream. My words—DIED, FIRING SQUAD—had tortured her further. But other words—brave, overjoyed, sing a song—had punctured her feelings like pins of joy, like a nervous resurrection of the soul. Maybe her soul was not dead. "Oh that sounds ... just like him, something he would do. What was the song?" She sounded jovial in a way yet I knew she was on the point of breaking, like the strings of a cello, stretched and stretched until BANG, they would all snap together.

"Yes! It was something very special and memorable, a poem about the soul." I said, then realising that I was making light of his execution as though it were a good event. "I mean, the singing and his playing ... that was special."

She looked around the room then. "But you didn't bring it ... the cello. I thought perhaps ..."

Now I was on my escape path from blame again. "I'm sorry. When you said in the letter that you hadn't got it back, it was a shock to me, because I did actually ask—and was told that—it would be returned to you."

"Oh, well, maybe it will." She seemed to have completely regained her composure, which was something that made me shiver. "Because that cello was him … it was his voice. When I get it back, I will be able to hear his voice again." Her head drifted upwards as if she was listening for some far-off sound.

"Do you play?" Her look stifled my voice. Then the look turned to pain. Absurdly, I thought it was sympathy for my pain. I was becoming acutely uncomfortable with my normal problems, which I supposed I should tell her about. Though they seemed so insignificant.

"Oh … I must show you around the house, some of his trophies and books and instruments. But none I must say is as important as his … that cello. We must get it back."

This was my sentence. We moved around the house slowly, and the rest of my leave began slowly.

I was locked in the house with this broken family with its layers of suffering and terrible silences. At night I had nightmares and flashbacks brought by guilt. But also lurking in my being were Cellos' mother's first words: "Benjamin, it's not your fault." I didn't know whether it was a pardon, but even if it was, given what she did not know, that could change.

There was little to do during the three days of leave. I walked in the garden, among the trees, like skeletons, until it begun to hail. We went to church, and I received a limp handshake from the pastor at the church door before leaving into the rain and hail. I was angry beyond words at the lack of any sympathy shown towards Cello's mother. But the anger did not really grow until afterwards. The vicar had probably done his "duty" when he first heard of Cello's death, perhaps visiting the house and bidding her to remain strong in her faith and in the love of God.

How, how, love! The whole concept had come apart in our hands.

I had no idea what the sermon was about. The vicar seemed like a tired officer urging us to continue with our life on the home front, "with the notable good humour of the British Tommy." I did remember that phrase as if everything was good fun in the trenches. Oh yes, it was all like a great picnic, a family picnic. And later there will be a family snap.

I burned with indignation as I suddenly remembered a photograph that had been taken of the battalion moving up to the line. That was before the whole Cello incident. We had been asked to smile and cheer for the camera and thought it was a good joke, as you would smile at a family picnic. The memory brought a bitter taste to my mouth, and had I not been in church I would have spat it out, spitting on the memory.

The RSM they had called the Old Man had been killed just after the photograph was taken. He was completely obliterated. They only found his boots with the feet still in them, nothing else. But the photograph they managed to print, and it got to the papers, we heard. It made us bitter, because the old man was killed because of it.

That bitterness stayed with us. We drowned it, of course, in rum. But it always came back. It wasn't only that. But now the whole falsehood came down to simple things, like Cello's mother and her questions that would probably never be answered. She was clutching at straws, but everything was cold, and there was no comfort from anything.

She had said that Cello's father would take the matter up with the War Office. He retired to a room in the house that I was not invited to and started writing letters, I assumed. I did not know to whom. We met at evening meal, but he appeared sullen, and I felt that he had dismissed me. Why was I there and his son not?

Men had hardly ever spoken of their fathers on returning from leave. Pride between father and son seemed to have broken. Though why should that be when sons were doing their duty? Mothers and lovers were the only links to the world beyond the army. But mothers lived in the past, and for lovers, there was no future. They wanted to forget the past. How could a man forget? How could a man plan for the future?

What future? What hope?

I spent a lot of time in Cello's room trying to read poetry;

> Though nothing can bring back the hour
> Of splendour in the grass, of glory in the flower:
> We will grieve not, rather find
> Strength in what remains behind;

These words that had seemed so noble seemed to lie dead now, as did all the other words that I had rejoiced over.

I was glad when it came time to leave. The goodbyes were haunted by the tragic, desperate pleading in Cello's mother's eyes.

But as I journeyed over grinding, smoke-filled hours, back to the hospital I thought of things that should have been said, arrangements that should have been made if I was to try and get the cello back. Nothing would satisfy Cello's mother, but getting the cello would bring back something of him, some link that I didn't understand.

Death in the trenches was such a normal thing. Cello's death was different and filled with injustices, some of which I could have prevented, maybe the death itself.

Could I now heal that injustice?

Chapter 13

I Scratch Some More Words
✳ ✳ ✳

Something awaited me apart from the leering taunts of the others—a brown envelope, an army letter.

> ARMY MEDICAL BOARD ATTENDEES; *Private Benjamin Routledge*
> HOSPITAL; *The Royal Herbet Hospital, Shooters Hill, Woolwich*
>
> *Date: 23 Feb 1918*
>
> *Private Benjamin Routledge is to attend the above medical board on the date above.*
>
> *Signed,*
>
> THE DIRECTOR OF ARMY MEDICAL SERVICES

This was expected. Everybody had spoken about it. The medical boards came every few weeks. What was to hold me back from a return to the front?

I had put on so many coats since joining the army, each one taking me closer to the possibility of death. You rehearsed the fear over and over, without talking about it, trying to find a coat to protect yourself.

Army uniform, equipment, overcoat in winter, steel helmet, rifle or Lewis machinegun, and bandoliers of ammunition. We also tried the coat of the drunken braggart. None worked. The soft mush covered by the coat never changed. The quivering and the hollow eyes, the terrible dread in the stomach and the breath of fear, the endless smoking. No coat covered them. Cello had worn that apron. I had worn Cello's dressing gown. His perceived cowardice was actually courage, but where had his coat of courage come from?

Cello's parents had waited patiently with the expectation that their son would return to resume a career that would lead to fame after a youth of endless practice and schoolboy awards and the loving nurturing of a rare talent. They now needed the courage to face that this had been taken from them.

Which coat should I take now as I faced the possibility of a return to the front? Should I just act like a sheep, bleating along, without even the hint of hope for the future, without a thought for the future, just accepting that this time, yes, *this time*, I would not come back? The rules of possibility and chances had to run out now. Would it be a dullard running to the rum, with trembling hands, then turning to the slaughter with a dead brain and a blank stare.

"I know I will die," one man had said, speaking of the possibility of going back in a moment of released emotion.

Or should we fight? I mean fight to stay alive, aware of some stirring within us, the unquiet human blood, daring to hope. Fight for what, what future! Cello's parents and my parents had shown me that even for the uninjured and untouched by the war, there would be no happy homecoming to resume a former life. Nothing would be the same, could be the same. What future was there? But someone was coming to my rescue at least in my mind. A letter awaited me from Midnight's wife. I had not forgotten her. I opened the letter with trembling hands:

> *Dear Mister Routledge,* (Perhaps it was time that we started calling each other by our first names. That would be a step loaded with messages that so far had been hidden thoughts)
>
> *I hope that your injury is not giving you a lot of suffering. My loss continues to be lessened by your letter. Now I must try to look to my*

future and build something without my husband. I have a wider family around me who are also giving me comfort, and I must be thankful for that indeed. Most particularly, I have a sister and brother (who I thank God did not sign for the war). They are part of the farming community here and are skilled at producing goods from the land, and we are in good living from that. They have offered me shelter as well as family security.

I have also received a letter from the British Army with some unpaid remuneration owed to my husband, which sadly he was not able to avail himself of to enjoy.

So you could say I am in a very fortunate position. But you know that a married woman who becomes a widow cannot become a single woman again. She has experienced something which cannot be undone, even though sadly I have no child to remember my husband by.

But I have to remember the fact that I have experienced the emotions of a married woman, and I thank God for that.

I hope to hear from you and wish you a very speedy recovery.

With all kind thoughts,

Joyce Pearl Johnston

My eyes burnt with the beauty of the letter. The handwriting had a physical beauty about it matching that of the words. I held it. Actually, I cradled it. It was longer than her last one. With shame, I realised I had not written to her even though she had asked me to do so. She was in another world, of exotic fruits and warm tropical rain and large green leaves—*green*. There was nothing green in my world.

Her letters brought her into my world though, and that was better than green.

I must write her straight away. I must keep her in my world, pathetic though it was, in comparison.

I found a couple of sheets of writing paper in the small drawer above my bedside cabinet and retired to the library. Before it was my sanctuary but now, maybe a waiting room for …

Dear Mrs Johnston, Could I perhaps address you as Joyce, if you wouldn't mind.

My recovery continues, and I am improving. Thank you very much for your letter, and I am sorry that I didn't write to you before. I got some leave from the hospital and had to visit the parents of a friend who also died. He was a cello player.

Now I have returned to the hospital and have been put on an army medical board. They may return me to the front as I now have a minor injury.

I was so sorry to hear about your husband. He was a great and brave man and a friend to me when I needed a friend.

Your letters are a very nice way to keep me going, and I like what you said about the land and your family. It made me feel envious that you are far away from things that are happening here and in the war in Europe. Families are being broken by the war, and fresh food from the land is something that never appears on our tables. It was wonderful to receive your photograph. But I wonder whether you have any more photographs of yourself and your family.

I pricked with embarrassment and premonition when I wrote about the photographs. I felt good taking the risk because I wanted a bigger picture of her. But I should have said more about Midnight. So many men were dying, it was something not to dwell on.

Thank you for reading my letter

I hope that I can now regard you as my friend and me yours.

Benjamin.

I had moved an ocean away from being her humble servant in my first letter. I had assumed to be her friend. I had used my name and hers. I had pondered over the first few and last few words for long moments. I read and re-read the letter before sealing it.

I had a sudden desire to see more of her place, her land, her country. I was aware of my own whiteness and frailty, my smelly, bent image, my fallen-in face sucking the life out of cigarettes, hooked nose like an old man's. I wanted to see pictures of the country where this woman who wrote these wonderful letters lived.

I needed a book with pictures, coloured photographs. School books of tropical lands filled a corner of my mind. Their interest was always fleeting. Now I had a reason. I looked around the library desperately. Where would I find such a book? My eyes scanned the shelves. In one corner of the upper shelves, I saw larger books with covers of shiny paper. I remembered from school that these were more likely to be atlases, and so it turned out.

There were colour plates. But only a few of these interspersed with the maps. It showed maps of the "colonies", with large proportions being red for the United Kingdom, including the island of Jamaica, which seemed tiny in comparison to its neighbours of Cuba and Haiti.

One coloured plate showed "a sugar plantation of Jamaica", complete with tiny black figures dressed seemingly totally funnily in a dress similar to those in another picture showing the "Nabobs of India". I replaced it and scanned the shelves for something more. My eyes caught a small, slim book in the same section entitled, "The emancipation of slavery in the Caribbean colonies." I took it down.

Slavery. In school, the tendency was to learn from a prescribed list of dates and events, without any human stories behind them. Yes, we in England were responsible for ending African slavery—we learnt that. We were the good, who had brought civilisation to the world and especially the colonies. In the trenches, we could identify with slavery. Midnight and I used the word and decided we were not slaves, as we were getting paid to be there, which ironically made it seem worse than slavery, as the payment was just a trick. It didn't give us free will. It didn't allow us to walk away.

As I opened the small book and flipped through the pages, I searched not for the facts bare and simple but for some sign of life. I had been given a life, perhaps two of them, my own improving one. Though the improvement was so slow, drawing the breath out of me, that I feared I would be linked to some disinfected institution for the rest of it.

As to the second life. I did not see her as one life. Her reference to family told me a lot. It comforted me but at the same time made me think that she would never leave her homeland. The book fell open in its centre, and there were several faded black and white pictures. People, at last, were there. I peered at them with excitement. This was a discovery. I absolutely could not help myself. I smiled. The people in the pictures were solemn. Some rode donkeys. Perhaps it had been raining for some seemed to have long raincoat type garments on. They actually looked like soldiers, for they seemed to stand to attention for the camera.

Then a sudden fear came to me. I did not know whether these were slaves or if they had already been freed. I searched the faces, hands, feet. They had a kind of shoes on. No, no. These were without a doubt *not* slaves. What had made me smile was their dignity. Freewill shone in a kind of fierce way. That was probably why they looked solemn. One held up a hand, waving to the camera. A slaves hand would have been shackled, and he would definitely not have held it up in a kind of salute to the camera. They looked like farm workers. Great leaves grew behind them, luxurious leaves like the green ones in the atlas photos. There was no colour to these, but still, they spoke of more life than in the whole of the gardens of this smelly hospital.

The people in the photos had thick black hair. Midnight's wife's hair had large curls, but this hair was so thick and matted, it was not really curly. But they were people, and she was a person, a real person who wrote such incredible words that I couldn't help but feel attracted to these people as well. I couldn't help but feel refreshed. It was a feeling that these people could somehow rescue us from the ravages of war, just as Midnight had rescued me. It might have been foolish but …

I put the book away.

I had my medical board to prepare for. I spent a couple of days in bed suffering from a bout of flu. Any minor ailment was made worse by your condition. I had a fever and felt lightheaded. I didn't read or go to the library. I did write a letter to Midnight's wife from my bed. Of course, the others in the ward became suspicious. "Writing to the lady friend then, Ben? When you gonna get 'er in 'ere? Get 'er to pay yu a visit. Sure she'd love that?" They cackled in a lewd way.

I sweated with the flu and was delirious at night. I couldn't remember the dreams the next day, but people said I shouted stuff and screamed. I was glad I didn't remember the dreams. Flashbacks were a regular occurrence for almost everybody.

The day of the medical board arrived. I was well enough to leave my bed. If I hadn't been, my attendance would have been cancelled. I didn't know whether to want that or not. I had to go.

Chapter 14

Good News and Screaming
✳ ✳ ✳

Never had I known expectation to be so changed as on that day.

There were three officers sitting behind a long table. It immediately reminded me of Cello's court-martial. Only one of them I recognised, the short one who brought our pay. They called him the Company Commander, but apart from the pay we hardly saw him. He was an administrator, not a doctor and certainly not a field commander. Company commanders in the trenches often came into the front line, sometimes more than the platoon commanders.

In the middle sat a lieutenant colonel who introduced himself as the CO of the hospital. I had never seen him before. He had no medals. The third officer I did know to be a doctor. Usually wearing a white coat, he was now in uniform also. He was a major. There was to be no medical examination of me on this medical board. Papers and files were piled on the desk in front of the officers. A woman, the matron, and a female clerk sat at a further table to the side.

The CO did the talking. "Private Routledge, we've reviewed your case. how do you feel?"

"I feel …" I didn't know whether to mention the flu. "I feel better, sir," I said eventually.

"How are you coping with your colostomy?"

"I can manage it, sir."

"I'm sure you can. However, as a general rule, it is not our policy to return men back to the front who might become a liability on medical services, and in your case that might happen."

I began to sweat more. Did that mean what I thought … ?

"However, there are some other matters in your case. He reached for another piece of paper. You were involved in an incident."

My thoughts flew to Cello.

He paused and looked at the paper in his hand.

"An incident in which you acquitted yourself rather well …"

I felt confused. "I'm not … sir." My mouth dried up.

"You protected your men with one other man while they withdrew, and you subsequently got your injury while withdrawing yourself."

"Oh … that, sir."

"Yes, well you have been awarded a mention, mentioned in despatches." My face must have looked confused because he explained. "It, it is an award, y'know. You will wear it on your medal ribbon." He looked at my tunic which did not have any ribbons. "You have spent the required time overseas, have you not? So you could be wearing your ribbon now."

"Well, sir … my injury … I haven't."

"No, no, of course, your injury, well. As I mentioned, we do not as a rule return men to the front who have an ongoing care need, as they might become a liability to the medical services. But in the fullness of time, of course, you may be able to return."

I resisted the subservient military inclination to say, "Thank you, sir." I remained silent.

So he continued, having cleared his throat. "We are building up the army for what will hopefully be a final push. We need experienced men to train that army. You have experience so we think you would be useful to help in that. So … also to help you in that, you have been promoted to corporal."

His speech ended with a resounding announcement.

It did something to me. "What about the man who got me out, who brought me back? He deserves something, doesn't he? And, and what about the other incident then, sir?" I said.

The three men at the table froze and looked at me. But the colonel only spoke. "I'm sorry you're confusing the issue now. I don't have any information about the man who, as you say, got you out … and what is the other incident you refer to? I have information about you only. The "mention" was put up by your regiment … er, the Worcester Regiment, along with the citation. This went to the army board for military awards, who approved it, and then to your regimental drafting office, who also approved your promotion. This all came to us here at the hospital, where you are currently serving, and we … I made the decision that you should not take up an overseas posting, and they decided to send you to a training unit, as I said …"

He got through his speech like a talking puppet, making emphatic speech emphasis particularly on the words *they, us,* and *we … I.*

I spoke without thinking. I hardly knew it was me speaking. "I don't care about they and us and you. I don't care about me! I do care about people who have died and one in particular who was *shot by you people!*"

I screamed out apparently at the end.

I sort of sagged in the middle like a rapidly dying flower, which encouraged the lieutenant colonel to address the clerk drily. "Get him a chair, would you?"

She did just in time. I sank down. The board was probably used to some soldiers breaking down when told they were returning to the front, although most would maintain a sort of quivering stoicism. But to be told you were staying at home and being promoted, which meant extra pay and getting an award all at once, would not normally be a reason for the breakdown, except perhaps a joyous one.

My eyes were blurred by tears, and I could not focus on the table with its three occupants. But of course, I could hear.

"Private Routledge, we are a medical board. We have other patients to see now, and as I mentioned, we only have information about your particular case regarding the aspects I have mentioned. As to any other, uhumm, areas of concern, these will need to be taken up with your Company Commander." He turned towards him. "Could you arrange an interview please?"

"Yes, sir," replied the fat officer.

"Good, well, Private Routledge … I thought we were to be the bringer of good news for you. I trust this is still the case, and I wish you the best of luck for your future." He nodded to the orderly, who stood behind me at the door and who now approached.

Pride made me stand on my own. Another outburst would have been futile. I was composed enough to realise that. I regained my feet and but did not stand to attention. I left without the assistance of the orderly. Outside, I realised I hadn't saluted either, which could have been a chargeable offence on its own as this was deemed to be insubordination.

At least it was in the real army. What army was I in now? Where was I?

I made my way back to the ward, down corridors and through doors that seemed strange and unfamiliar.

The ward was full of expectation. "Come on, Ben. Spill it to us. Spit it out, you dodger. When you going back?"

I stood in the middle of the large room, as though on the parade ground. When you don't have confidence, a large space brings fear. It would have been better, far better, had I been going back. But now ... now I suddenly hit the floor.

There was laughter because they had heard that, in fact, I was not to go back. That I was to be promoted and that I was to be decorated. I came out of a momentary blackout still on the floor, to the sound of laughter. The orderly had followed me and spread the word, with a furtive whisper. I tried not to cry. But I still had difficulty standing, and of course they laughed even more to see me. I was doubled up. So I crawled to the bed.

Then came the hatred. I felt afterwards that a man could be killed by hatred. A terrible sneering bullying hatred. It didn't have to be physical.

It did almost become physical when a letter arrived a few days later.

The orderly handed out the mail. "And one for Private, or should we now say *Corporal* Routledge. Oh, look at this stamp." She peered at it. "Jamaica ... so, friends in faraway places. Here you are then."

She thought it would be exciting for us all and that the other patients would join in my pleasure, like one big happy family. We were far from that, but when she held the letter up so that perhaps I would run and get it and another patient, already out of bed, stood and almost ran around the bottom of his bed and snatched the letter, she didn't mind. He scurried back to his bed, almost opposite mine.

The new owner of the cream envelope; he had a stomach wound like mine but hadn't had the infection and seemed to recover quicker, held it up in a kind of triumph. Then he looked at it suspiciously. "Who's it from then, Ben?"

"It's private, ain't it?" I shrugged as if in a kind of indifferent manner not as a child might do, demanding his things back. But I felt like a child, a cheated one.

"It's a lady, Ben, ain't it, your lady friend? She on holiday or someut?" he was genuinely puzzled. Jamaica was somewhere he had no idea or notion of. It could have been Southend, which was the place Londoners went on holiday. Or if you were rich perhaps Brighton. But the stamp made him suspicious, although he appeared to look at it without seeing, because I could see from my bed that it had a picture in green on it, not just the king's head, like ours. He was more interested in the contents.

"Come on, Ben, we all men. Can share our lady friends, can't we, eh?" he wheezed. The other bedridden occupants wheezed with laughter. A lot of wheezing went on in this ward, laughing, coughing from cigarettes or from lungs damaged by gas. Still, most were almost guaranteed to go back to the front. So their attitude towards me could be excused.

I did not count any of them as friends or comrades demanding some loyalty, as you might have had in the trenches. These men seemed to be of the bullying kind, and they were about to torment me.

The one holding the letter, a small Yorkshire man was getting braver. His name was Len, and people regularly made up little rhythms about us, Len and Ben. But neither of us enjoyed that, as we weren't friends. Though he laughed more than I did. He enjoyed a crowd pleaser. Playing to the crowd now, he reached for a table knife that was on his bedside table left over from lunch. With a broad, toothy grin, he cleaned it with his tongue. Then, showing the knife up and around and the letter in the other hand with a flourish, he slit the envelope at its top. Had the knife not been there he would probably have handed the letter over to me, but it was easy to open now and remain in effect unblemished. Letters were inevitably torn open by hand.

Now, having laid the knife aside, he dangled the letter with his left thumb and forefinger. "Come and get it, Benny boy then," he goaded in a singsong voice.

The others took up the refrain. "Go and get it, Benny boy then."

Lenny led them again. "Come and get it, Benny boy then."

They replied even louder. "Go and get it, Benny boy then."

Len became more provocative and bolder as the song grew louder.

He turned the letter with the slit downwards and, holding it with both thumbs and forefingers, he began to sway it backwards and forwards like a pendulum, at the same time tilting his head this way and that in time with the swaying, his grin getting bigger.

A square of paper dropped from the envelope and fluttered across the central corridor between the beds coming to rest on the polished wooden floor approximately in the centre. The song stopped abruptly, and heads turned and craned. "Ahhha." The grinning Len stopped grinning.

"Hey, look!" cried another voice.

I was leaning back in my bed, and I could not have even begun to get there. The injuries of others seemed to disappear.

"Get it!" shouted someone from further away as four men dropped to the floor and scooted across.

One man made it. He was a quiet one but was acting under Len's influence. He picked up the square. "A photo, look," he said and started grinning anew. He carried it to Len, his kind of mentor, and passed it over curiously and unquestioningly.

Len took possession of this new trophy with a kind of reverence. My privacy had been breached, and there was no going back. It was open house. My new status as a corporal meant nothing. But he had discovered another reason for the torment. After studying the picture while I looked at the white reverse side, he slowly raised his head, and instead of a grin, cracked his face into a kind of grimace. "He's only gone and got hisself a *dirty darky.*" He spat out the last two words. His face came up and extended out. He leaned forward, and his neck became like a snake bringing the face further towards me. His eyes bulged with hate.

I often thought afterwards about that hate and why it was there. What gave rise to it?

My first thought was the coward's way out, denying any knowledge of the letter or the picture. There must have been a mistake in the address or something. But I had been a coward. Now it was time to be a man, as Cello had been a man and Midnight. So I gathered my strength and stood up from my bed. I walked with some difficulty but finally managed to stand at the foot of his bed at the place where the doctors and nurses stood. "She is a woman, not as you described her," I said, "and I would ask you to give me the letter and the picture. It is not your business who I write to or who writes to me." I didn't hold out my hand.

He looked at me and withdrew his face, shrinking it back to its normal position. He took the hand holding the photo down to his bedclothes, to a safer place. "And what are you going to do about it, Benny boy?"

I took a couple of steps around the side of the bed, still keeping a safe distance from him. "Well, the action is in your hands, to return my letter and photo."

"Well, you never had it in the first place, did you? So it's not really a case of returning it."

"It's my name on the envelope." I didn't go along with his question-and-answer game.

"Oh, is it and what about inside then? Are you sure the letter is for you and the picture? Anyway, who is the lovely lady? Can you not share that with us?"

"As I said, it is private."

"Yes, but Benny we are all mates here. Anyway, you are not a *private* now, are you? So are you going to pull rank on us now, *Corporal?*" He grinned his ghastly teeth.

The whole ward waited.

Chapter 15

I Read Out Loud
*** ✳ ✳ ✳ ***

I don't know what made me turn away. I was not afraid of the hate in his eyes. But I did want to question it. "You are not worth pulling rank on. It would be wasted. But why are you so interested in a picture of a woman." I suppressed the anger against what he had called her: "a dirty darky".

"Well, Benny, ordinarily, as I said we all mates and we would have shared a photo and had a laugh, but come on *that* photo, *this photo*." He gingerly brought it out and started looking at it again, this time with more concentration, as he seemed confident that I would not attack him for it. "This woman is … is." His face became distorted, and the hate came out of it again.

"She is a Jamaican woman," I said simply. "She is a coloured woman from Jamaica. She was married to a Jamaican man who saved my life."

I walked with difficulty back to my bed.

"Saved your life?" The concept seemed to be a bit difficult for him to accept. I had not talked about it, though the others seemed to have told the story of their injuries endlessly.

"Yes, saved my life, after I was hit with this. He dragged me back to safety as the section withdrew with the Boche after us. He gave me her address, and I wrote to her after I was evacuated, just to say thank you. She told me he got killed."

Everybody knew that black men from the colonies had volunteered. Some were even formed into separate regiments. My story was simple and often repeated. The wives of men who had been killed often clung to a friend who communicated with them. If that man had also been killed, the women would be broken, as they had sometimes lost brothers as well. But something about this did not seem right with Len.

"She is not like you, though, is she? So why would you take a woman, a coloured woman, as your lady friend?"

It was pointless for me to deny that she could be my lady friend. "Well, she is not my lady friend at the moment, but why should she not be?" I was in bed. We all were, which made it difficult to hand back the letter and the photo, although a bigger issue seemed in question now, and a point occurred to me. "If men both white and black can fight together, why can't white men and black women become friends?"

I had almost won them with the story of Midnight saving me and then being killed. But this was beyond that, way beyond. Of course, Len was the spokesman.

"A white man should never have a coloured lady friend. It's never gonna work, never." The hate was back in his eyes.

"Why?" I asked simply.

After a pause laughter erupted. It was nervous laughter from some, wheezing, forced and unknowing laughter. So the question was unanswerable and therefore would remain unanswered. We could go back to the letter though. Now they had a sort of secret power over me. They knew my story, but also that the ending could never be a happy one. So they could play with me.

"Okay, read the letter to us, then," said someone from a different bed, his curiosity getting the better.

"Yes, Ben, you can have it back so long as we can hear it. That's fair, ain't it?" Len had softened his hate somewhat, perhaps at the prospect of more embarrassment on my part.

It was sealed. Ordinarily, this would be a subject to share and laugh about. Even once when an older patient had been visited by his wife we had joked about their lovemaking in the bed almost in full view of the rest of the ward. His wife had become a kind of family to us. But this was different. She was different. She could not come into a room and sit with her husband by the fire and join with his fellows in food or laughter.

Even injured as we were, we could not be the fellows to her husband. Her husband could not be our fellows.

What if I were to be her husband?

Well, then I would be cast out, away from the fireside of normal life. The false bravado of soldiers had brought us together, but in real life which must be faced after a war, however impossible that might be, unwritten rules take over. The war will not take away those rules; it will add to them, make them more unfathomable, more carved in stone. My parents showed me that. Cello's parents showed me that. The chaplain at Cello's mother's church showed me that. I could not think these things at the time. It was only my desire to read the letter that drew me up. So I shrugged appearing to make the whole thing trivial.

"I will read the letter," I said.

"Yes, you will read the letter," came the sneering reply.

"So, give it me then."

"Well, we need some reassurance that you will read it, don't we? Tell you what; I know you want to hear the letter. I can see it in your eyes. So you don't have to act all indifferent about it. I will give you a page at a time. There are two pages here. She is obviously interested in you to write a two-page letter, eh? If you don't read it, you don't get the next page. That's fair, ain't it?

"Why are you talking about being fair? It's my letter. That's not a matter for discussion, is it?" I said, but the fight was leaving me.

"Of course it's your letter, Ben. Okay, here you are. Here's the first page. Read it out. He held out a page. I took it and went back to my bed with it.

Once there I looked at it. It was the same copybook handwriting. So I just began to read in as matter of fact way as I could.

"Your letter heartened me greatly. I am glad that you want to write to me. As I said before it has helped to cure my loneliness.

"My family continues to be a great comfort to me. I think we all have need of family ties and I hope your family supports you in your injured state."

"Wait, do we not have a salutation to hear?" queried to the obsequious Len. "How does the letter start? Is there an affectionate address, perhaps, 'My dearest Benjamin', or some such?"

"No, just 'Dear Benjamin.'" I omitted to say that she had added a note agreeing that we should drop the formality of addressing each other as Mr and Mrs. This note alone made my heart jump a little.

"Oh, really? Well, carry on then." He settled back in the bed.

I paused before continuing. *"You mentioned going to see the family of another friend who was killed, a cello player apparently. You are obviously a good and kind man. This was a generous act and cannot have been easy for you. I applaud your efforts, which I am sure were appreciated by the family."*

Here I had to pause as my eyes were welling up with tears. I had struggled with the concept of irony at school, but it seemed that me being a "good and kind man" for visiting Cello's parents was totally ironic when it was me that had been a cause of their pain in the first place. Eventually, amid the expectant silence, I was able to continue.

"I have enclosed a photograph of yours truly." I paused in confusion. I already had her first photo securely hidden. But this phrase was a casual reference to the photo of the sort that posh English people might employ, not Jamaican wives of Jamaican soldiers. I looked around for the photo, but it was not forthcoming from a grinning Lenny. So I continued. *"It is not the best one, but my mother likes to keep photographs of the family, since they are few. It was taken after I completed my studies at Kingston University. My marriage prevented me from continuing with my studies, but I am hoping now to resume them."*

I had reached the end of the small page, written on one side, so I looked up, and this time Len was holding up the photo. His face was expressionless. There was a sort of bored dismissal of the secrets revealed already in the letter. He turned the photo around in his fingers then swopped it under the bedclothes for the second page. Another patient got out of bed and scurried around as a messenger eagerly delivering it. This page was more densely packed with neat handwriting.

"I hope that you are managing to occupy yourself in hospital, reading and I'm sure studying as well. It is a way to overcome all afflictions, and for me, it also helps my grief, because I know my husband would wish me to better myself. It would make him proud.

"Perhaps you could share with me your observations on this matter; though of course your convalescence and recovery is the most important thing by far on your mind. I am fearful of a return to the front for you. All men must do their duty, but this must be a heavy burden of expectation for you to carry, along with your injured compatriots, of course.

"Well, I fear I am running out of space. It is so good to be able to share thoughts with another, especially one like you who will know my grief and its depth. But my recovery is proceeding and God willing it will strengthen. So now I will leave you with kind thoughts and the best of wishes for you, your injured compatriots, and of course your family.

Squeezed in at the bottom of the page was an after note. *"I would much appreciate you addressing me by my middle and favourite name of Pearl. Thank you for asking this. You are a well-mannered person."* She signed the letter, *"Pearl"*

I did not read the after note out.

Silence fell on the ward, like one that I had experienced several times at school after a deep dressing down at the assembly from a headmaster frowning above his bow tie in the moment before the foot shuffling started.

In this case, a slow hand clap from Len's bed broke the atmosphere.

"So, there you are. Now you can give me the photograph," I said. Then I added, "Or if you don't, that won't make any difference either." I shrugged in dismissal. Her words gave me the confidence to do that. Her words drew the conflict out of the situation like lancing a boil. I folded the letter and put it under my pillow as if burying a piece of treasure. The paper meant nothing. The words which now lived with me were the treasure.

Later I found the photograph pinned to the ward notice board with a drawing pin through Pearl's face. Someone had found a pen and inked a question mark at the side of her head. I took down the photograph with some difficulty, noting that my fingernails were dirtier than they should have been.

I needed to keep my hands cleaner to live up to her words.

But I was alone, scrubbed or not.

The name "dirty darky", used by Len when he saw the photo, had hurt me so much that I sought refuge in the *Oxford Book of English Verse*. It seemed to come from a sort of gutter poetry, words that might be included in a jeering trench song. Her words seemed beautiful, as poetry should be, like flowers. I found Shakespeare, the dread of all schoolboys, especially those contemplating the army.

> Shall I compare thee to a Summer's day
> Though art more lovely and more temperate:
> Rough winds do shake the darling buds of May.

The sonnets spoke of love and flowers, unlike the plays, which did at least offer sword fights and battles.

I read William Wordsworth, whose "Daffodils" brought mocking laughter from schoolboys:

> I wandered lonely as a cloud
> That floats on high o'er vales and hills,
> When all at once I saw a crowd,
> A host of golden daffodils;
> Beside the lake, beneath the trees,
> Fluttering and dancing in the breeze.

Flowers did not survive in the trenches.

A cello and its weeping and moaning did. That sound stayed with me.

It had moaned on the day they shot Cello. On the day that poem came to my being.

Out of the dark that covers me …

These were fitting words. But Pearl's were like those that a female poet might write. I looked for female poets. They seemed added at the end as if in an afterthought.

Love was, of course, a theme of much poetry. But as I flipped through, picking like a bird, the word "Mistress" seemed to have some prominence along with flowers. One double-page spoke of tulips, the dying rose, a primrose: *"Cherry-ripe, ripe, ripe I cry, Full and fair ones come and buy."*

This was too much for my exhausted and weak frame. There was something like heaven about it all. As if love was a paradise full of enchanted flowers and sun-kissed daffodils, where men and women danced and sang and were forever happy.

Such could not be the case.

I flipped back to the female poets. One poem hit my eyes.

ALICE MEYNELL
Renouncement

I did not know what renouncement meant.

> I MUST not think of thee; and tired yet strong,
>   I shun the love that lurks in all delight-
>   The love of thee- and in the blue heaven's height
>   And in the dearest passage of a song.

These words caught me a little, for they seemed to speak of the yearning that was creeping upon me, although I didn't admit it. Also there was the reference to a song, which brought back memories of Cello yet again.

I continued on with the poem:

> But it must never, never come in sight;
>   I must stop short of thee the whole day long.
>   But when sleep comes to close each difficult day,

Yes, my fellow casualties would certainly see our relationship as something that should never happen. But in the end,

> With the first dream that comes with the first sleep
>   I run, I run, I am gathered to thy heart.

Of course the bed is a private time of thought in which fantasies become a reality and all have a happy ending. But dreams did not; most were terrifying relived moments or heartwrenching regretful ones.

I drifted towards sleep. Cello's poem was ever present:

> Beyond this place of wrath and tears
>   Looms but the horror of the shade,

The "shade," night, or death possibly.

Yes, night was a horror despite thoughts of Pearl, whose small and damaged photograph lay beneath my pillow while the other photo was in a book on my bedside table.

If morning brought sunshine, then hope could begin again. I was desperate for paper to reply to her letter. For once I had something to say that didn't need to be forced.

Dear Pearl,

Thank you for your letter and of course the photo which I treasure. It is lovely. You are a very intelligent person. I have not been to university. I am a common soldier. But I have been trying to study and read like you said. The subject I have chosen is poetry.

I expect you enjoy poetry yourself. It sounds by your letter that you might. Some of the things you say are magic, as some poems. It has been giving me some comfort, and indeed I have been looking for poems written by women which I have found a few, including one by Alice Meynell, which I really like.

I had chanced on the way to talk about love without even mentioning any feelings for her. By now I was sure that somehow I had love.

We have a library here in the hospital, and I use it. I am the only one. It gives me some peace from my fellow patients. There are a few poetry books. I had one book which I used, but I did not wish to lay bare my limited grasp of the subject.

If you wish I can write some of them down for you.

When I wrote this, my heart gave a jump. I knew the ones I would write would be love ones. I moved onto more ordinary subjects.

I had a medical board which has cleared me for home service but not yet overseas. That is good news I suppose. I still do not know what I will do or when I will leave the hospital. I still have some medical problems and will never be fit like I was.

Yours forever,

Ben

I sent it and immediately regretted the dismal end and the signing off with "Yours forever". I was trying to say something that would show I was educated, but it was a false show. The poetry was real but so limited, like a child with a new toy, the only toy. "Yours ever, old girl" had something of the officer class ring about it. The truckload of officers sweeping out of the logistics area with a raucous song after Cello was executed, going to sweep ladies off their feet.

Black ladies? Definitely not.

Everything seemed impossible and any thought of love or poetry, foolish and unreal.

Reality was my bag of excrement, smells of disinfectant, the moaning voices of bedridden, the sharp voices of nurses, slow figures in striped pyjamas, quick figures in blue and white, beds and boredom.

My future sat in my mind like an oncoming train journey, but with dread. After the visit to Cello's parents, every journey seemed a joyless prospect.

Chapter 16

A Shaft of Sunlight
✳ ✳ ✳

I was waiting. That's all a soldier can do. He has no power to bring his future to fruition. It is always in the hands of others. I had been promised an interview with the Company Commander. Eventually, I was summoned and told I had to wear a uniform. What else did I have to wear, or should I go naked?

I walked across a kind of square surrounded by the windows of wards, towards his office. I imagined eyes watching me. I did not look up towards the windows to meet the eyes.

"Come in, Private Routledge."

It was an office overlooking the square. His had been one of those set of eyes. How wonderful this must have been to some officers looking for a cushy, blighty job. Or perhaps he was bullied about it in the officers' mess. Probably not. It would have been an accepted part of life. Perhaps some mild ribbing by the officer patients would have happened.

He was reading a file, my file, I supposed. I waited at attention having saluted on entry.

"Stand at ease, if you would. Now …" He looked up at me with a sort of vacant look. "Are you all right, Routledge?"

"I believe I am on the mend, sir."

"Good, good … but if that is indeed the case, why are you behaving in the manner you displayed at your medical board?"

"I was referring to something what happened before I got injured, sir.

When a member of my platoon was executed for desertion and … well, it shouldn't have happened … sir."

"A great many things have happened in this war which should not have happened, Routledge, but we cannot undo them."

"Yes, I know that, sir, but this affected his parents in a terrible way. It was an injustice. His parents were not even told of his execution. I told them. He was a cello player, and his cello had not been returned to them."

"*A cello player!*"

"Yes. He played it before they shot him. I was his nominated friend. He played and the firing squad sang a song. Then they shot him."

The company commander's face grew red, then pale, then red again, as if his emotional reactions were changing before my eyes. "Are you telling me that a condemned man played a *cello* before his execution?"

"Yes."

He grew more incredulous. "And that the firing squad sang a *song!*"

"Yes."

"What officers were present?"

This caught me by surprise. Then I remembered the platoon commander giving the orders to the firing squad. "Yes there was a lieutenant in charge of the firing squad."

"A *lieutenant*, nobody else?"

"I don't think so, no."

"Was there a padre?"

"I do not remember seeing one."

"You said you were his friend. Did you attend the whole of the court-martial?"

"Yes, I did."

"Did you give evidence?"

"No, I didn't."

"Why not?"

"They never asked me to."

There was a long pause in which the officer seemed motionless, looking at my file. "Courts-martial are not my specialty. I know little about them," he said. "But this one and particularly the execution seems bizarre. You were obviously affected by it, so would you like to tell me more about it."

"Well sir, the court-martial just went by without me knowing really what was happening until suddenly Cello … was sentenced to death. I suppose I thought that justice might happen. I didn't know what would happen. I thought it might all … be turned back somehow."

"So how do you think justice did not happen then?"

"Well, the full story did not come out. It happened so quickly there was no time …"

"And what was … the full story?"

It was a casual question, asked rather impatiently and therefore without the invitation to spend time telling the true story in full.

"A casualty was screaming in no man's land. We were sent out to find him, and when we did, one of the patrol just shot him. Cello didn't agree with that and threw away his rifle and ran off. He joined the Germans and helped collect casualties. But eventually he came back and was charged with desertion."

It sounded so ordinary, so insignificant. I looked out of the window when saying it not at the company commander. There was a long pause before I finally did look at him. He was looking at the file.

He looked up. "The casualty, perhaps he was beyond help. Could you have got him back?"

I paused. He hadn't even asked whether he was a British soldier. Surely that made a difference. I didn't mention that we had no stretcher. I began to think about the screaming—eventually, it had been crying—for his mother. He was English. He had been one of us. I felt as though I was going to collapse again as I had in the medical board. But this time I was more prepared. "May I sit down, sir?"

There were several spare chairs in the office. This would have been unheard of in a barracks environment, a private soldier asking to sit down in an interview with an officer. But this was a hospital. So he waved at a chair. "Take a seat then, Routledge."

"Thank you, sir." I sank into the nearest chair having turned it to face the desk. Finally, I admitted, "It would have been difficult to get him back … yes."

"Things happen in battle, bad things, but your duty and that of your cello playing soldier is clear."

I had a sudden feeling in my throat as if a bundle of wire wool had to be vomited out. "Duty, sir, but I beg your pardon. Duty was never clear.

We obeyed orders. We did our job. But duty … is that not deeper? If you think something is wrong, do you have a duty to do it? We talked about this in the trenches quite a lot." My mouth was extremely dry, as it always gets in battle.

"If I give you an order to do something, you do it."

"Of course! My job is to obey orders … but that is also on the assumption that the thing you are telling me to do is acceptable to some moral values. For instance, if you ordered me to kill myself, I think I would be entitled to say I cannot do that." I felt suddenly almost lifted from the chair with a power far beyond that of my station. The things I was saying were not the things expected of a common soldier. But then I had been there at Cello's court-martial and his execution. I would never be the same again.

The weather had been cloudy as I walked across to the office, but now some clouds had cleared, and a shaft of sunlight suddenly shot through the window. It fell between my chair and the desk behind which the Company Commander sat. It bathed him in a sort of pale light where dust particles danced in a permanent suspension. Then the sunlight seemed to catch him in the eyes, and he blinked. He leaned back to try to get out of the glare. But he could not avoid it.

His desk was brown and heaped with brown files. A faded leather panel in the middle was barely visible. His Sam Browne belt rubbed on the front of the desk as he moved his stomach, which appeared rather overfull of officers' mess food.

My old wooden chair squeaked as I moved. My uniform hung around me. A man lost about two stone in weight when he got injured. I had not put that weight back.

The loss of eye contact through the sun's glare diminished the officer's power. He seemed to drift away on a haze of dust in the sun's rays. Then as if from far away, he said a very strange thing. "Many groups of … soldiers in the past did not allow their casualties to be taken prisoner, and those injured would be killed before that could happen. Also, I believe some groups of soldiers in ancient times did commit mass suicide. I would have thought some of them might have been ordered to take their own lives."

Suddenly I began to sweat. I thought of my weaknesses, my lack of energy, and my habit of catching fevers, my bag of shit hanging heavy at my side. Eventually, I was able to mutter a reply. "Sir, we are not in ancient times now." Unlike in ancient times, there were some rules and laws of war now. I knew this somehow, but I didn't mention it.

I remembered Cello's outburst at his court-martial. He was talking about the justice of killing in war. As it was a legitimate part of war, there was no justice in war, and therefore the court should kill him there and then. They didn't, but a few days later the firing squad did kill him, confirming his statement that justice was no longer valid. I continued as best I could. "This is a modern war, with mass, senseless killing, where humanity seems to have departed ... But Cello showed us some civilisation, a spark of civilisation, and something that showed he was just. We needed to hold onto that idea. We lost it in the trenches. I had lost it in my mind for much of the time. But it gradually came back ... is coming back."

I had no idea where this speech came from.

The officer sat back out of the sun's glare, into a shadow. "So, are you saying that this man, this cellist, was more civilised because he played the cello?"

"Not because he played the cello. Well, the president of the court seemed to think so, because he had a sort of strange mental attack when he heard that Cello was an actual cello player and he shot himself."

He sat motionless except for the rapid blinking of his eyes, seeming perhaps unable to take in this information.

I continued. "When he first arrived, as a re-inforcement, he was a figure of fun, of ridicule, because he was different. There were three of them—musicians, I mean—supposedly from the "Artists Rifles". Yes, they were sort of innocent. We had lost so many men, so many. They just fed men forward to the battalion, any men, any cannon fodder as we saw them. We didn't really see them as fit to fill the boots of the dead and injured. Then they re-badged them to the regiment. Not that any badges arrived, so they were different, not of us ... our tribe."

The officer reacted. "*Tribe*! It was a regiment of the British Army, the British Army, with all its tradition and values."

"But it didn't have the identity of the regiment that we started with when we went up, because nearly everyone changed as people got killed or injured, and new men even if they were in the regiment, didn't have the same feeling for it. So we didn't see ourselves as a regiment anymore. The replacements came from everywhere. Only a few came from the depot. And what values there were in the regiment could not be transferred to them. The only thing that could be transferred was our loss of every civilised value and our instinct to kill or be killed."

He shifted uncomfortably. "But *tribe*, I don't think so. Doesn't speak of very good discipline within your battalion ... How was the discipline? Or perhaps you are not in a position to answer that." He repositioned the hierarchy again putting me back in my lowly position.

"Well, I am ashamed of my part in Cello's incident, and I believe we could have changed the outcome of the court-martial. So from that respect, yes, our discipline, my discipline, was poor."

He looked hard at me, trying to fathom what I had just said. Did he see the irony in the notion that more self-discipline on my part would have led me to stand up more determinedly in Cello's defence?

"Well, we can't change what happened. But I do admit that there seems to have been some strange goings on with the ... um, er court-martial and firing squad event. There will be records of this, and those should be available."

"Sir, for me there is one thing that I need to do or needs to be done by somebody, return the cello that was used by Cello—I mean, Private Harris—to his parents. That is what they want ... desperately."

"Well, it should have been returned with his other effects. Not sure why that didn't happen!"

"It didn't, sir."

"And you are in touch with the family."

"Yes, I ... I told them he had been executed. They didn't know."

There was a long silence in the room. Even so, the enormity of that piece of information did not invade. Nothing could recreate those moments sitting with Cello's parents. Nothing could describe my feelings or begin to understand their feelings.

"Yes, difficult, no doubt. Well, I can do some searching, some enquiries. Would that help?"

"Yes, yes, it would, sir." I was on the edge of my chair now.

"But ... in return, you must try to settle down and realise that you have a good future in the army, actually preparing them to win and end this war. That is what you want, isn't it?"

"The end of the war. Yes, of course, sir."

"And for us to win, Routledge."

"Yes … sir."

"Good, good, so can I take it that you accept your promotion and your appointment to the depot for training duties? This is a great opportunity for you, you know. You need to grab it."

"Yes, sir," I said meekly, sealing my fate.

"Good, good," he repeated absentmindedly. "Well, the process now is that you will, at some time in the near future, receive your discharge from hospital, and you will be drafted to the regimental depot." He searched the file briefly. "Yes, Bordon, I think, or you may go to another depot. You will be informed of the date, and that is where you will go, as a corporal. Your duties will be training new recruits."

"Do we have any of those, sir?"

"Pardon … what do you mean, Routledge?"

"Well, I would have thought the country would have run out of new recruits."

He looked at me hard again. "Well, there are young men coming of age all the time, of course, and others are signing up who previously were in so-called protected industries, as women take on more roles. Then, of course, the Americans are apparently coming, though not, of course, as our recruits."

"Yes."

"We are going to win, Routledge, you know."

"I'm sure they will, sir." I distanced myself, rather like an observer on the touchline than a player on the pitch.

"Well, if that's all, I think you have everything you need to know. So it just remains for me to say, good luck. You are lucky, you know."

I stood. "Yes, sir, thank you. But please can you try to find out about the cello?"

"Can't promise, but I can try."

"Thank you, sir." I saluted, turned, and left.

As I walked across the square, something made me turn back towards the office. The Company Commander was standing at the window looking out towards me. He had seemed trapped behind his desk. Now he was trapped in his office. I blinked and understood something that Cello had passed to me: freedom. But the officer looking out at me was not free.

I turned and carried on walking.

Chapter 17

Hatred and a Typed Letter
✳ ✳ ✳

I returned to face the hatred that was becoming more solid since I had started to move around and out of the ward on "secret" missions.

"More secret interviews then, Benny boy. Who was it this time, the Fucking Commander in Chief?"

"Just the Company Commander."

"Oh *just* the Company Commander, just the Company Commander. So fucking high and mighty now, aren't we ... with our fucking little darky lady friend."

"Lady, huh?" piped up a wheezy voice. "Darky women ain't no ladies in my book. More like fucking whores."

I rounded on him and tried to make a threatening fist. But I was not up for a fight.

More provocation came from a further bed though. "Yeah, but with this whore, you would want her to be paying you. 'Ud never pay for fuck with a darky however desperate us was."

"Oh, I dunno. You don't look at the mantelpiece while you stoking the fire, do you?" responded the wheezy one.

"No one gonna look down there at that though, are they? Not black and dirty like that."

The hate-filled jibes came back to Len. "Yes, I'm interested, Benny. What is it like, you know, down there, on 'er? What is it like when she opens em up? Wouldn't want to be doin' it in the dark, would you? You gonna miss everything."

"You'd be all right. The smell ud lead you to it."

Hideous forced laughter from almost every bed followed.

I headed for the lavatory, determined to get to the library after that. I wanted to gaze at Pearl's photos, but my every move was being monitored, and I was afraid my mail would be intercepted.

Later I asked the sister to bring any letters for me direct to my bed rather than hand them out with the others in the middle of the ward.

"Oow, you're lucky," she said. "I've just got one for you here." We were outside her office. Her door was always open, unlike the Company Commander's office, which made me worried. She casually opened a drawer and took out a small bundle. "We were going to give these out when everyone was back from their afternoon smoke." Leafing through, she selected one. My heart was pumping. Then it fell into a small pocket of anxiety; the letter was not from overseas.

"Thank you, Sister," I said.

I knew that the letter was from Cello's parents. I had a sort of dread in opening it.

Dear Mister Routledge,

(I knew straight away that this was Cello's father not his mother writing. The letter was typed.)

Following your visit we have been trying to find out some information about our son's demise from the War Office. Of course we had no reason to disbelieve what you imparted to us. But I'm sure you will understand that we wanted to hear it ourselves from an official source. Of course the War Office did eventually confirm what you told us. This gave us yet more pain as you can imagine. We had held out some hope of, as we discussed "a mistake". Sadly this was not the case.

Thereafter we have tried via other departments within what I suppose could be described as the English War Machine, to find out more information. I have to say that our efforts

have been almost entirely fruitless, which can only add to our misery.

However, in response to our plea for Marcus's effects including his cello, we finally received a scruffy parcel with items of his uniform inside and a handwritten note saying "deceased effects", followed by his name and number in different handwriting. There was nothing else, no letter or personal note and no explanation of anything.

I fear that this uniform, which has blood stained bullets holes in it, is all we have. The uniform is labelled with Marcus's name, which we assume was written by him. This is our link, our only link, to our dead son.

Needless to say I sent a letter straight back to the War Office thanking them for the effects and stating that they were incomplete as they did not include the cello, our son's most prized possession. Also stating that we had no information as to the whereabouts of the body. Unlike for many soldiers obliterated by shell fire or other battlefield weapons where no body can be located, our son's body would have been completely intact and presumably has been buried locally in France. His whereabouts is a matter of great concern to us now, and we hope that eventually, we will discover this information, though as yet I have received no reply to my letter.

As to the future. All I can do is to keep going in my endeavours to discover something, anything, that might help us overcome our terrible void of grief and shame. It is something that deadens everything else in your life you know. Whatever else you have is nothing compared to this. Our lives are nothing now, nothing at all. I have to keep going so that those in high power may sometime in the future realise that there are people connected to those killed in battle, however they meet their death. Those families or people linked to the world outside this war are real.

However, your life is hopefully getting better. Your recovery will make it so. We hope that you can still help us in some way, though I do realise that you are but one small part of the war machine, as I mentioned. It is devouring us all now in one way or another, and it will change us all. Nothing will be the same ever again.

Yours truly,

Robert Harris

I could not hold the letter for long. It was a dead weight on my heart as well as my hand. But I managed with somewhat shaking hands, to fold the heavy sheets of paper and stuff it into its envelope. I placed it in my bedside locker which was becoming a sort of drawer within my soul.

What could I reply to this letter? What could I tell them? I had no information to impart. My piece had been done, like a loathsome actor in some tragic staging. Now I had sloped off to some pathetic corner to mope and snivel. My only hope was to return to them bearing the cello and a true story. But truth and resolution of anything seemed too distant.

And from Pearl, no letter.

Perhaps my expectations had become too great. I had enough experience to know that a man who waits for a woman could wait for ever. But against that, a man who appears too eager or rushes into something he thinks is there for the taking may soon find himself empty-handed as the woman of his dreams takes flight. Perhaps that is what love poetry is about, the fulfilment of fantasy in words rather than actions. There were actions at nights: with a pillow the only bedfellow, or mistress.

I had to turn my attention to my future employment.

Other letters to do with this seem to flood in. Not all of them were addressed to me, but I was kept updated by my favourite nurse. There was a discharge form, a drafting letter informing me of the depot address where I should report and when, a month from now. Then almost immediately another drafting note for a different depot. All seemed confusion in the army administration. It set me up with some nervous sweats and sleepless nights. I was granted leave prior to reporting for duty. Where, though, was a mystery and where to go on leave was a question.

My confirmation as corporal and details of the new rates of pay arrived. For newly promoted corporals, it was 1s 9p per day. That was enough for a quart of light ale in some pubs. Perhaps the Castle Tavern, where I had stopped on my journey to Cello's parents, it would be somewhat less. I recalled a notice board of prices, which seemed to have been altered, probably on a regular basis. There would not be a free issue of rum at the training base unless the weather was particularly bad. It was never as bad as the trenches.

All these miseries made my stomach twist more in anticipation and resignation of the road ahead: the soldier's road. I could numb my brain and do the things that were asked of me, and yes, I had a lot of knowledge to pass on, a lot of knowledge. Not all of it was for passing on.

Stupidly I had been waiting for a letter from Pearl. But now I had so much to tell her that I could write again without risking a feeling that I was pushing myself onto her in a romantic way.

Dear Pearl,

I hope you are well. I have some news about myself and will be released from the hospital and go to a training job at a garrison. I have been promoted to corporal. It is good news, I suppose. I will not be going to the front again. Perhaps the war might be over before they send me again. Obviously, that is something everybody would like to see. But who can hope? There is little hope in anything here, particularly not in a hospital.

I think I will go to a depot called Bordon, near Worcester. But the date should become clear soon.

I am looking forward to getting out of hospital, but I will need to get fit again.

I will write to you again when I know when I'm posted.

With every nice thought,

Yours,

Ben.

I thought long about the end. It sounded silly when I first wrote it. But I was not an accustomed letter writer, particularly not to a lady who seemed so tender and intelligent. I was a man and had to act like one. I had enough weaknesses in my body but must not seem weak in spirit. I was happy that the end did not show how nervous I was about the posting confusion.

As always my writing was a scratchy imitation of her beautiful hand. Sometimes I imagined her writing her letters to me. Her dark hand slowly moving across the page just below her breast moving slowly up and down with her breathing. Perhaps she was sitting on some veranda overlooking bright green banana plants with their great luxury leaves hanging down. I thought of her being lonely. But then with a pang of nervous tension, I saw men approaching her, men of her own colour. They would be laughing and beckoning her to come down to the fields of bananas. Of course, she was a widow. But still, the men of her own colour would be strong and muscular. And they would be smiling with white teeth. My skin was pale, and my teeth were definitely not shining white. The thought of me taking my shirt off in front of her was dreadful. Even more so the thought of my waist, around which hung this bag of shit.

You stupid fucker! You shit bag, I told myself.

There was also a creeping idea that seemed to overtake my thoughts in the day. I could not get a woman here, so I would need to be satisfied with a woman from the "colonies".

In my night time, the thoughts were different and of course centred on the deeper mystery of her private area, of her jutting breasts, which I tried to see from the photos she had sent. Of course, the blouses were high collared and revealed only a barely noticeable curve. But they were of a woman quite well endowed. That was certain.

I did not write to Cello's parents. The task seemed too great, and I had nothing of interest to tell them.

My letter to Pearl crossed with her reply to my earlier one, which was to give me new strength, something I was badly in need of.

Chapter 18

Am I afraid of a song?
✳ ✳ ✳

Fever always brought extra dreams. During the early part of my hospital treatment, I found myself often losing my rifle and trying to fight without one. There wasn't a fear of the enemy in these dreams, but of self. Some shame always hung like a curse. Something was not done. I knew what it was now but the dreams continued.

I would be taking Cello's body somewhere, perhaps to hide or bury it. Bits of the body came away in my hands. Laughter could sometimes be heard. And of course, I would see the eyes. They were never dead. There were oceans and rough seas, which I took perhaps to be the trenches and the area between, where bottomless valleys whispered safety then promised drowning if I should venture there with my burden.

One dream, perhaps the only peaceful one, never repeated, saw me at the helm of some swift sailing ship making effortless way up a wide river. Mist obscured the water's surface and the banks of the river. Actually, they might not have really been there. In the end, the ship drifted to a stop, and I floated safely down to … wakefulness. Dreams never had a true ending. Someone in the ward said that if you stayed asleep to find out the ending of a dream, you would die in your sleep.

Men did die in their sleep, of course, or at least at night, but whether they were dreaming or even asleep was not clear. It was probably more fortunate if they were; otherwise, they would die in pits of misery and loneliness. The night in hospital was always long and always lonely.

126

My situation brought new dreams to accompany the fever brought on the nurses said, by my anxiety. For some reason, she casually mentioned this to the whole ward. My fellow patients not yet exhausted of their bullying made up to song.

"Oh poor little benny, he's so scared. He's not going to the front,
he's not going to fight, he'll be in his bed every night.
He'll be ruling the roost with tapes on his arm
In his very own farm
But who, who whose the chicken now.
Puck, puck, puck egg, who's the chicken now?"

(Repeated time and time again with gestures of flapping wings)

When they got fed up with this single verse, someone added another.

"He's got a dirty secret. He can't tell his men.
They're fresh from their eggs,
They're new recruits, but even they won't be
scared out of their daisy roots
To hear his lady friend's as black as coal
And doubtless, it'll cheer their very soul
To hear that he, he, he's the chicken now
Puck, puck, puck egg, he's the chicken now.

(Two verses seemed enough to be repeated over and over)

The mention of soul, of course, set off my chain of memory back to Cello's song:

'I thank whatever gods maybe for my unconquerable soul.'

My soul might not have been fully unconquerable yet, but it was on the road.

My new fevered dreams seemed to go further back, with my thoughts, to a time before all this.

March 1916 had brought conscription. I had resisted signing up before. Had I been in a factory or municipal environment, peer pressure would have brought the early enlistment. But I hung onto my measly "apprenticeship", to a design office. That was what it called itself, although designs other than for the war effort seemed pointless after 1914. So eventually I surrendered, without choice, of course, and without special passion for a cause, "the cause".

YOUR COUNTRY NEEDS YOU.

Lord Kitchener's pointing finger had left me shrugging with a sense of indifference that my parents seemed unable to understand. "Suppose it's about time you did, lad," said my father in a lame way. He had no passion either.

"It might do you good, Benjamin. Maybe meet a nice ..." My mother had some romantic idea of war.

"He's gonna fight, woman, not philander."

This word from my father brought a silence to the front room.

But philandering, or "tart sniffing", as it was more usually referred to, was a favourite occupation of the training days before we were finally shipped to France. Although only in conversation, as we were allowed out only once in every four weeks. And those excursions to a public house would usually end in a brawl rather than the company of a tart.

"They're all giddy jilts any road," said one of our corporals, which was supposed to encourage us back to our task in hand.

Those endless days of drill, bayonet practice and shooting occupied some of my dreams.

Someone once hung an old waitress's dress on one of the bayonet dummies. We plunged into that one with more glee than the rest, until an officer called it profane and unwarranted and had the waitress outfit removed, by which time it had grown false breasts and a blonde wig.

We started using the word *profane* in our everyday language. "You're a profanely bad shot, Private Ben Routledge."

Yes, I was not good on the range.

Women were part of the dreams, as was shooting. But you never quite made it with the woman, as you never quite hit the bull's eye. Actually, there was no bull's eye. It was all about grouping your shots into a small space. But being left-handed impeded me, as I was never issued with a rifle with a left-hand bolt so I could never settle into a decent position to get my shots tight. I always had to shift my right arm, to work the bolt, and this unlocked my grip on the rifle.

When it came to the trenches, this did not matter. You didn't worry about grouping your shots. Just shooting was difficult enough.

About my life before, there were few if any dreams.

Pearl's letter fell into my dream- and fever-filled state. I was impatient for news of my draft and constantly searched the ward doorways for some unchanging step of a nurse or hurried message to be imparted to me. But the life of a hospital grinds on tediously slowly until an untimely death stirs staff into urgency, by which time it is often too late.

Perhaps the nurse who brought the letter I awaited had learnt that I was a victim because of them, so she brought it silently to my side and slipped it into my lap. I seized it into the folds of my uniform. Those of us destined for discharge were ordered to wear the uniform now during the day and sit doing "meaningful military tasks", which included reading the new infantry training manual. Much had changed. A new army was being made, and I was to be one of the cooks.

There was physical training too, which for me was a very unjoyous thing, as it involved shorts and a sort of vest. But there was no escape.

But all that was as of nothing compared to the letter. Freedom also gave us more ability to escape our fellow patients. There was a dining hall. Nurse/waitress service was at an end. We were nearly independent.

This was a long one so I settled myself in some corridor corner where I believed I would be safe.

My Dear Benjamin,

I have to first apologise for the delay in replying to your letter in which you mentioned your love of poetry. This made me so excited that I had to go and look up some of my old school textbooks to be sure about certain things. I too am a great admirer of poems and poets. At school, I tried to write some poetry myself, but I'm sure you would not want to see my efforts against those of the greats that you discovered in the Oxford Book of English Verse. I have actually found a copy of that in our local library here and have been reading the poet you mentioned and others.

You may be aware that Alice Meynell is very active in the Suffragette movement. I admire her for that and all the other women fighting for their right to vote. Of course, we here in Jamaica are very far from that as voting is based on land ownership and is open only to men. But we pray that at some time this will come our way after the lead set by those courageous women in London.

I have also been looking up the stories of another of my favourite artists, Pamela Colman Smith. She is a true storyteller and artist who illustrates books and paints and writes. In fact, when she was only eighteen and living here in Jamaica, she wrote a series called the Anansi Stories, which she mostly got from Jamaican mothers and grandmothers. She was the first to write these down.

But I believe she is now living in London. Some say she is a woman of colour, that is, a mixed-race woman. But I don't believe that, although I would like to meet her and find out. I have actually written to her. I was such a lover of her stories!

But I suppose nothing will come of it.

I would though love to visit London.

I'm sorry, I've run out of paper. But I will try to write again to catch up with all the things I want to say.

Yours ever faithful,

Pearl.

Was this a love letter?
Was it a letter to a friend about poetry?
Was it both?

Women were a mystery to men; that much I already knew. It was that mystery which sometimes turned to fear and then perhaps hate, as I had experienced here in the hospital.

The women's suffrage movement. Men mostly laughed about it. Husbands knew about it, as their wives pecked them with it or mocked them. "When we get the vote, you will be out of a job. And I will be getting paid for doing everything I do around this family," one patient had quoted his wife as saying.

But then I read the letter again and "I would love to visit London" hit me. I rocked back in my chair. But warmth suddenly spread across my heart.

Could it really be that this woman, this black Jamaican woman, could just climb on a boat and visit London? Would she have the money for the fare? As my daily pay hardly extended to a large glass of beer, this seemed ridiculous.

Just as ridiculous was that a woman who might have those means should write to me. But her means in one area was clear. Intellectually, she was far superior to me!

You stupid fucker, you shit bag, I told myself. I gripped the arms of my chair.

"'Course, they never mean what they say" had been another wise pronouncement about women.

Well, in fact—and here I had to go back to the poetry by women—the few remarkably intense poems about love. Maybe they meant more than they said, or meant it differently. So just as I had talked about love poems as a way to express my emerging ... attraction, for her, she might have talked about visiting London to see *me* rather than follow her dreams of seeing her childhood writing heroine or join the suffragette movement.

Another snippet from the front room conversation after I had announced that I had signed up came back to me. "Well, it'll make you a man, lad!"

So why did he continue to address me as "lad"?

But now yes maybe it was my chance to be a man. Not in battle, although some would say my Oak Leaf "mention in despatches" sort of medal proved that I had done that. But the greater test of truth and courage with Cello's story had yet to be addressed on that score.

Chapter 19

Words Are Fired but Miss Their Target
✳ ✳ ✳

It was to be Bordon Barracks in Worcester. It might have been Aldershot or even Plymouth, but I had a final interview with the Company Commander, who confirmed it and handed me my drafting order.

The interview seemed a continuation of the last one as I asked if he had any information about Cello, with the Company Commander seemingly concealing something by an uncomfortable body movement in his chair and the Sam Browne belt rubbing more on the front of his desk until the buckle got caught under the desktop preventing him from leaning back. Then he pushed his chair back with an angry scraping on the wooden floor.

I broke this discomfort by handing him the letter I had received from Cello's father. "I received this from the man's father, sir."

"Ah … hum, urhum. "He read it through slowly, coughing to fill the vacuum of silence and cover any embarrassment. "Well, of course, courts-martial are well documents events—have to be, legal business very important. Taking a man's life in the name of justice, difficult decision to make, very difficult."

Something in my brain blurred into a red ball. "Taking a man's life in the name of justice." Who had shot the casualty? Was it Jack or the corporal, who had made that decision, that casual decision, that "very difficult" decision? But this time I was able to keep my voice calm. "Yes, sir, in the cold light of a court, it is perhaps a difficult decision. On

132

the battlefield, it is a decision made on instinct, on self-preservation, on survival, even shooting a casualty, not on the balance of justice."

He looked at me intently. "And your point, Corporal Routledge?"

I now had my formal promotion authority though not the actual tapes, which I would get at the uniform store after this interview and have them sewn on by the ladies who worked at sewing tables in the back of the store. "My point, sir, is that ... that same instinct and actually self-preservation made Cello throw away his weapon."

"How? I don't follow you."

"It's a complete overturning of the order of life, isn't it, sir? War, I mean. So how can the normal rules of justice apply?" I was tempted to add, "For gawd's sake, you fat idiot," but if I had, I would have gone straight to clink myself.

He posed himself carefully, aware of the gravity of the moment and perhaps aware that no sergeant major or even witness to our conversation stood by to take matters further. "Well, as I recall, we did explore this theme during your last interview."

"Well, yes, we did, sir, but I do think it was a different aspect. Here you mentioned how difficult it was for the court-martial to make a decision about taking a man's life 'in the name of justice', and I was pointing out that decisions were made by all parties to the event but others were made in a moment on a battlefield when instinct and survival were uppermost in the men's minds including Cello, and these things should have been taken into consideration by the court instead of the simple facts of whether or not the offence had been committed. Because in that situation, justice as we know it, ceases to exist. So how can it be applied in the cold light of a court-martial?"

This time it must have been his turn to see a red ball or perhaps two, for they appeared on his cheeks.

"That is precisely the point: *because* of the conditions in battle *justice* must be strictly observed."

"I would venture to say that *because* of the conditions in battle that justice must be tempered, or should I say made easier."

He looked at me for a long time—well, it was probably a fraction of a second. I knew I had not captured what I wanted to really say. I had not captured it at all. Or if I had, the words had fallen on deaf ears.

"Easier? Well, I doubt that will win us the war, but we were speaking of the letter, and I have had the chance to look into this a little since our last interview. It so happens that I have a friend who works in the relevant War Department office in London that deals with courts-martial reviews. All cases have to be reviewed after sentencing, and records of this are, of course, kept …

"The case of err, Private Harris, of course, was reviewed. I can tell you that the review did not reveal anything unusual about it … I did mention to him your story of the cello playing and singing, and he knew nothing about it. I have to say that he, like me, was somewhat shocked by it …"

He shifted in his chair but this time with a little more confidence in his final pose.

"I think I would put this down to an internal matter dealt with at local level by the military police. I don't think any official report would have been made about it."

"But the accident involving the president of the court was of course unfortunate." He had tripped onto this subject like a train going over points at a junction, effortlessly, with only the change in sound to give it away. I stood to attention. There was no chance of a chair on this occasion.

"Yes, sir," I said hopefully.

"But these sort of things do happen, unfortunately, and sadly, senior officers have met their demise in this way," he sort of barked, as if speaking above the sound of the train going over the points.

In a sudden flash of inspiration, I replied, "But I would have thought his next of kin would have been very distressed in the same manner as Cello's parents."

When I mentioned the name Cello, he seemed to flinch, as if he knew that I held the name out of something that had grown into love though it might have started, at the very beginning, as derisory. But now mentioning a senior officer's next of kin in the same manner as a soldier's seemed to unsettle him as well, as if the two sets of people were from different planets. "After all, they both have to suffer the same loss, don't they?"

"Hum umm! Well, I suppose you do have a point," he grudged. But he did not make the point, which was probably in his mind, that the death of a convicted deserter by firing squad should not be treated with the same gravity as the death of a senior commissioned officer. Their worth was incomparable. But then ... but then ... the senior officer did suffer some sort of madness, which indicated that he, at least in that moment, saw Cello as a special case. But perhaps not in the way that I was trying to describe to my Company Commander.

Our conversation seemed to hit a brick wall. But he did have some brighter news for me, perhaps cruelly leaving it until now. He picked up the letter again, scanned it momentarily, and looked up. "I believe the body will have been buried locally. That would have been ... The body may have been moved, but it is the intention that all bodies, how so ever they met their death, will have their locations recorded for posterity. So the next of kin will be informed of this fact, may already have been." He looked at me, as if landing a heavy defeat on my armoury of inadequate vocabulary with its onion layers of meaning, never reaching a bull's-eye.

And of the cello itself. "Well, I fear, you know, soldiers are great ones for collecting mementos of the battlefield. Of course, I wouldn't say this to his parents. But I do fear it will have been picked up by someone, not probably one of the firing squad, which I'm sure held respect for ... um, Private Harris." He couldn't summon the courage to call him by his nickname. Then in a final assault, he gently delivered his death blow, like a slow, silent bayonet. "But you were there, so this is something you could have done yourself."

His victory was assured, but I did not leave the office crushed. I had remained standing, and I knew my ground. I knew my failings also. I had been over them many times in my mind.

I did go to the uniform store and found I had to pay for my stripes as well as having them sewn on while I waited in shirt sleeves and braces. Not the honour of presentation on a parade in front of regimental ranks, the oak leaf pinned on your chest by the colonel, a handshake, the band playing while parents, wives, and girlfriends looked on in admiration, never that. Rather, a full-length mirror in a dark corner, where I looked at myself and checked the positioning of the stripes. If they weren't right, it was not the lady at the sewing machine put on a charge by the regimental sergeant major at the depot where I was about have a new beginning.

First were the goodbyes and final medical and letters and leave.

Chapter 20

Leaving
✳ ✳ ✳

Hospital has a droning monotony about it, which we were all sure prolonged the injuries suffered by those inside. The aim was to leave, but was it? No one wanted to go back to the front, but in private, some did just to get away from the place. Because some feared the nursing staff had a secret desire to keep the hospital open for as long as possible to keep them in work.

I had seen outside. There was a bustle about the town. Well, it was close to London. But in that pub, those prices, very few people could afford them. And my father's scoffed answer about draughtsmen. "Ha, those sort of people will be walking the street without a farthing in their pocket when this is over." Something like that.

Women needed to work. They couldn't rely on a dead husband or an injured one or a totally well one trying to get his old job back. The world would be different. Women might have the vote. Yes, the war would end one day. Most thought it would be soon. Most thought we would win. We needed to train an army for the final push to victory. Or was it too late? For some strange reason, an anxiety began to creep into me in those final days at the hospital that I might be going to miss that. Perhaps I was returning to my old self, the Ben of bravado and a kind of indifference.

The rum would beckon. The free rum would not be available, so another source would be found. Was it needed? No, I wouldn't be returning to that Ben.

The difference Pearl had brought into my life hit me every time I looked into the mirror. Would she want me? I noted that my hair had taken on more lustre. It hadn't had any before, but now? I did wash and brush it more. It was black, and some even had at some time looked at me believing I was part Italian. I had even thought of using something like moustache wax to give it more of a shine.

The face underneath was still pale and hollow. I wanted prominent facial bones, not flat ones that made my nose appear bigger.

I would grow a moustache, of course. In the hospital, we were encouraged to be cleanly shaven because facial hair was considered unhygienic and could conceal more injured tissue for facial wounds. But for a corporal at the depot, moustaches would be mandatory. No doubt some would attempt to match the Regimental Sergeant Major. He might look suspiciously at them on parade and whisper under his breath something like, "Appropriate facial hair, Corporal, if you don't mind."

"Very well, sir" would come the immediate response, and action would need to be taken before the next day dawned. The RSM was the only non-commissioned officer to be addressed as "sir". Though those of non-commissioned rank and age approaching his would be able to relax this rule, especially in the sergeant's mess.

I seemed to have grown into my rank before officially taking it up. Perhaps that was why they promoted me straight to full corporal, not lance corporal. The single-striper did not retain a great deal of respect unless he did the job of a full two-striper, which many did. Otherwise, it was a thankless task and ranked with jobs such as supervising the digging of the new latrine, which Midnight and I had managed very well on our own.

But I was to discover other tasks and changes to the whole of the way a platoon conducted themselves in battle, and I was to be one of the ones teaching those changes.

I thought I would receive a letter from Pearl in answer to the one that had crossed her last one to me, in which she spoke of her joy for poetry and desire to visit London. But I was not worried if it did not arrive before I left, as I had great confidence in the postal system to forward my letters on. But I did need to write to her and tell her of my final posting news.

Dearest Pearl,

My final posting has arrived, and I am to go to the Regimental Depot at Bordon in Worcester. I am feeling a lot better now and am hopeful of passing my final medical to get my release within the next few days.

Don't worry if you have already written to me here, letters will always be forwarded on to a new address, but I am now a full corporal also so you can address me by my rank when you do write. Anyway, the new address is: Bordon Barracks, Worcester, Worcestershire.

Anyway, I shall take some leave before I go to my new posting and will go home to visit my parents. I am sure I will write to you from there, as I won't have anything to do and will be bored. I shall probably go to the library.

I liked what you said about your love of poetry. It is so good that we have something in common. You said that you would love to visit London. Of course, I would love you to come, but you know that everybody says, oh there's a war on, what can we do? Nobody has money, and Army pay is very small, and I don't even have civilian clothes. I might try some on when I get home on leave, but none of my old ones would fit. I have lost weight and don't look very good.

So please think of me for my good fortune and my luck. I am so lucky to have a job which is safe from a return to the front even though the money is so small but for all that I am in quite good spirits.

Yours ever,

Ben

Where was the love now? My letter seemed dead. What had happened to the excitement? It was there in my night time, but here on the paper, where was it?

Perhaps the poetry, Cello's song. I had stopped going to the library, as I had to prepare myself for military service instead of hospital service.

I sat out on one of the long verandas outside the ward overlooking some garden as I wrote the letter. It was, of course, spring by now, almost exactly one year since the whole Cello thing had happened—one year! Most of the time had been spent in bed or sitting somewhere like this.

Men had come and gone. Even Len had gone to another hospital. Those able to manage crutches moved on quite quickly to "rehabilitation centres". Exercise was the accepted way to get disabled men back to a near normal life now, and many would be fitted with artificial limbs. Those terribly afflicted with facial injuries might never be able to leave a hospital. What a life they faced, except many had no face and often no eyesight or speech. Who knew of the hearing? What world's did they inhabit? What a legacy of the war.

The lucky ones! Voices echoed so often in your head, from the time of injury to evacuation, snippets of conversation heard. "He'll be off to blighty now, lucky bastard." "No bloody use anyway."

"Hope he drowns in his own shit!"

But "lucky bastard" was the most often heard or expressed, either in jealousy or genuine appreciation of the "luck" befallen you, as being still alive.

This is what sometimes made me feel Cello was the lucky one. He had done what his soul wanted to do at the end, played his cello and prepared himself for death. Many patients had cried so much at the thought of going back to the front. Those that did were handed the cruellest of cards. After being so "lucky" to get injured and come home, then struggle to recover, what was their reward? Return and face death again.

"I know I will die if I go back." That was the view of so many. A lifeline had been snatched away.

Nurses comforted many, their only comfort. Even the ones with bad facial injuries begged to go back so that they would die rather than face a life after the war. Some had their wish granted. After some had been returned, people even asked about them. "What happened to Sandy, the one who lost his chin?"

Answers were never forthcoming. Stories were told of men who got injured and came to this hospital, returned, got injured again, and came here again and then were returned again to the front with tears streaming down their faces. Perhaps this happened as the hospital was close to the dock where many ships arrived.

This hospital, as boring as it was, with weeks and weeks of monotony, showed what war was. War was not the broken bravado that all the patients seem to aspire to, to get back to, although they didn't want to go back. But there was a kind of terror in the thought that there was nothing else. But the hospital showed the reality and result of the war.

I knew all this now. Cello's parents did not know. But what would they care? We were still lucky in their eyes.

Cello's father's letter still added to my lingering shame.

Then in my preparations to leave, a time when all thoughts of fever attacks were put to one side, and our physical exercise programme was stepped up, a letter arrived that shook me from my self-pity.

My dearest Benjamin,

I have both joyful and desperate news to impart.

Let me start with the desperate. I am not sure whether news reaches you in hospital. Perhaps you have access to newspapers. Have you heard stories about how black American people are being treated? Benjamin, it pains me terribly to say that they are being horribly persecuted by some elements of the white population, particularly in the deep South, which was of course previously the place where slavery was most in evidence. The Civil War was fought to end slavery, but it seems there can be no end to the suffering of my people.

Whether they are being blamed for the economic ills that now seem to be threatening that area, no one can tell, but some rage against them has boiled over into murder. They call it lynching, where a group of people take the law into their own hands and decide to punish those that are perceived to be responsible for "crimes". But these are not crimes proven in a court of law, and often they would seem to be merely an expression of anger by black people against the way they are being targeted.

But it is the nature of the so-called punishment that is the most terrible part. Men and women are being taken and hung, tortured burned to death, and even disembowelled while still alive. Is there no end to this madness.

There is even a report of some men who are returning from the war being taken while still in their uniform. How could this be done to men who are fighting for their country?

I find it difficult to write about this. I am sure you as a good man will find it also a truly unedifying story. So let me move onto my joyful news. You remember me telling you about my childhood author heroine, Pamela Colman Smith who wrote a series of stories about Jamaica. I mentioned that I wrote to her. Well, she has actually written back to me, YES, it's wonderful and heartening, but what is even more exciting is that she has actually invited me to stay with her in London. Can you believe this? This could be the answer to my dreams. Dare I say it to OUR dreams. We will be able to meet. I cannot tell you how joyful that makes me feel.

So with the benefit of her letter of invitation, I can book a passage to London. Of course, I will need to find the money for this, but I am sure my family will be able to help me.

Oh, Benjamin, I can't wait to see you. I have a picture in my mind of you. It's not a real picture, but your goodness will shine through and make you wonderful in God's eyes and so in mine.

Please write soon, and tell me you are happy with my news, and of course I will tell you as soon as I can of my planned journey.

Yours ever faithfully,

Pearl

Her writing was so neat and close; otherwise, the letter would have run to many pages, but she packed the words onto the paper. By the end, my heart was on fire.

Once I had read the letter again, and again my face began to prick with embarrassment at the thought of that she was trying to get away from America to come to Britain, where she would face hatred again because of her colour. Of course, I had not told her of the way they treated me in the ward because of her.

She did not live in America—I knew that—but I sometimes slipped into the thought that it was all part of the same area of the world, although it was not an active thought. But they were all tied up in slavery—that much I did know. So I believed that she might be at risk herself from this lynching. I could not make the horror of what she had said penetrate my brain.

I had to protect her. That I knew as well. I had failed Cello. In a way, I had also failed Midnight. In dark moments, I believed I should have protected him, even though I was the one who got injured. He protected me.

Now his wife depended on me.

I would love and look after her. I felt a certainty about it all. The woman, a strange woman, no doubt, Pamela Colman Smith, who would be a suffragette as well, had offered her accommodation.

I did not feel opposed to women as many men naturally did. "A woman's place is in the home." I did not feel that. Pearl's independence in some ways excited me. That is what made her determined to come to London.

The night I got the letter, I prayed silently about her. I mouthed such unfamiliar words. "Oh, God, don't let her get lynched. Please, please, God, keep her safe. And God, please bring her to London."

I thank whatever gods may be for my unconquerable soul.

Let her soul be unconquerable, oh God. Make her soul strong. Make my soul strong also.

I burned under the sheets.

You thought war made men bad. You thought that on going home everything would somehow be better and thoughts of war would be something to laugh about over the bar in a pub: a continuation of the bravado turned to back-slapping memories and happy thoughts of survival.

No. Things could be even worse now. Well, America could be, and then it might come here. Or more likely Jamaica.

Oh God, oh God, please protect Pearl, I prayed. I had never prayed like that, not as a child or in the trenches. Never.

I slept. I didn't dream the night after I received Pearl's letter about the lynchings.

I had things to do. For my medical, I stood naked and pale with my bag hanging around my waist and got looked at and prodded by a nurse and two doctors. "Breath in, deep breath!" She screwed up her nose, obviously thinking she smelt something terrible, something worse than fresh excreta overflowing from the bag, which it wasn't. There was always a bit of a smell of the bag and disinfectant but not usually anything else. Although as one patient had helpfully pointed out to me shortly after the first operation to fit the thing, "You can smell your own shit when you leave it in the bog, but you'll get used to it when you carrying it around. You won't smell it. Everyone else will, though."

The doctors seemed satisfied, and white coats turned to check patient documents and signed me off as "fit for home duty".

I posted final letters, which included one to Cello's parents telling them where I was to go, and of course I wrote to Pearl. I had already told her of my posting and the barracks address. I hesitated to tell her my parents' address and in the end did not. But I did tell her that I had prayed for her and that her safety was my most treasured concern. I told her that I would joyfully welcome her to London. I did not tell her that getting leave to meet her would be very difficult. This worried me.

Everything seemed so unreal. I was in love with a black woman. Or was I? Would she come to London? Would it all be a dream and disappear on waking?

I said goodbye to the nurses but to virtually no one else. I walked out with my small case and uniform in a kit bag over my shoulder and took the tram to Woolwich. This time I had made sure that I would take the train from the Arsenal station. I would not pay a return visit to the Castle Tavern.

Chapter 21

I Impart My News and Find a Book
✳ ✳ ✳

My noise shaking journey took hours. Whistles and smoke getting in my teeth and up my nose, corridors and compartments and banging doors were my travelling pals. As usual, the world was on the move. People looked at each other. Women were travelling alone. I didn't travel before the war. Most of these people probably wouldn't have done either.

Stations and stamping of warrants, taxis; a raised porter's arm, a uniformed arm. Uniforms were the order and the way things were ordered, each with its own importance. Out to the small gravel road at the back of the station, reminding me of the square where they shot Cello. "This way, sir. Won't be a moment, sir. Home on leave, is it? Have a good rest. By golly, you boys deserve it, all of you." After a few minutes, a black taxi coughed into view. Before 1915 it would have been horse-drawn. "There you go, driver's got the address. He'll get you home safely," followed by a salute.

Off we moaned, the new form of transport with an old engine dragging. I had dreaded this: going home.

I had decided to get it off my chest as soon as possible.

"Benjamin, my boy." At least she had put the gloves aside. But she wiped her hands on her long skirt when she wasn't wearing an apron.

"Welcome home, lad!" A hand pump from my father.

The routine would be similar to hospital—meals, time spent in each other's company, and bed.

After the meal on the first day was to be the time for my announcement.

It was a meagre meal, a few small pieces of mutton with thin gravy, over-boiled potatoes, and cabbage.

"You go ahead and I'll join you in the front room."

Front rooms were an expression of class, or in this case aspiring class. My mother aspired to a higher class. Many soldiers would not have had a "front room" or a back room, just a room where everything happened, including the baths, which had a scullery off with a cooking range or a stove and sink, and perhaps a clothes mangle. No toilet would be inside.

We had a front room, as did Cello. My father wore a suit to his train-movements-management work. My mother called it management. That was his uniform, a manager's one. But after the war, when troops were no longer travelling by train, would he have a job? Would he have a manager's job?

This terrible prospect hung over my father and mother like the teetering, moss-covered brick wall at the back of the house.

Before that, he had worked for a printing firm. He wore a long brown coat but underneath a shirt and tie. So, in my mother's mind, he was a manager there as well. But he did spend time on the shop floor, with the working people. That was how my mother spoke of them—the working people, as if a manager, by position, had no work to do.

She had secretly wanted me to be an officer. Perhaps she thought then I would have no work to do, no responsibility to take.

But I had disappointed her. Perhaps I had disappointed my father as well.

That aspiration to a better class must have been communicated by me to my section and definitely to the other patients. They had been a crowd of ruffians, without any regimental identity to bind them or us as a group. One asked me once why I talked so posh.

Going to the library was apparently posh.

I sat on our bare dark sofa in my uniform with its creases of travel and smell of train smoke. I had no belt or cap on, but my regimental collar badges and white embroidered corporal's stripes stood out. I had cleaned my buttons before leaving the hospital. The clock ticked loudly.

It was a warm April evening. Easter had come and gone. I had prayed but not gone to church at the hospital. A chaplain came in every Sunday including Easter Sunday, but I had missed it.

"So, finally a promotion. Good for you," said my father.

"I'm so pleased you are not going back over there," said my mother, but she didn't sound as though she meant it. She sat upright in a long skirt and cream blouse with embroidered collar. Expressions of affection were not a thing she seemed to indulge in. However, she did insist on my education being proper, as she put it. So I suppose I had to thank her for my love of books and the "Invictus" poem and the trips to the library to see other poetry, perhaps even for my ability to engage Pearl in some meaningful conversation. Although letters were different from conversation.

"Yes," I agreed.

"You must rest and get strong."

"What are you going to do over leave?" asked my father.

"I have some work on my military manuals. The army has changed. And I may write some letters."

My mother brightened. "Oh letters, may I ask to whom?"

"I have a lady friend now," I said very simply.

"Ah!" my mother stiffened. "A nurse. I thought as much."

"Not a nurse. She's a woman, a woman from abroad."

"Oh!" Her hand went to her mouth seeking the romantic ideal. "Is she French? Did you meet her out there?"

"Not French. She is from Jamaica. She is a black woman." I saved them from having to draw the conclusion that as Jamaica was peopled by mostly black people …

This time it was my father's turn to react. "How on earth … ?"

The sentence was finished by my mother. " … Did you meet?"

"We haven't met yet. She is the widow of the soldier who saved my life when I got injured."

Sitting with my parents, I felt a calm certainty about my lines. "I love her," I said. I felt a small guilt for not talking about how Midnight had saved me. But there was always a sense of exhaustion about telling the detail of what had happened because disbelief was always the reaction.

"You haven't met, and yet you say … you love her, *a black woman!*" my father erupted, as I knew he would.

Suddenly I was back in Cello's parent's front room, trying to tell them of the death of their son. This seemed almost as painful for my parents.

But why should that be? I felt an anxiety attack coming across my heart. But I tried to remain calm, as I had known this would come.

My mother seemed to have strangled herself. She was inhaling deeply, but as her hand was across her mouth, this must have been difficult. Having stood up suddenly, my father then sat slowly back down. He started shaking his head.

"No, it can't be. It's against the law, the law of this country. We are English here. We are ... we are ..."

"White. Yes, we're white." I helped him out. "But I served with her husband. I got injured, as you know. He saved my life. I wrote to his wife, as he had asked me to do, and found out he had been killed. Then Pearl and I became friends through letters. Then we became more than friends, and now she plans to come to England. When she does, we will meet. After that, I don't know what will happen."

"You mustn't meet. You can't."

"And why not?" I turned my full attention to my mother.

"Oh, Benjamin, you wouldn't understand. How could it be possible?"

Then my anxiety levels did boil over. "WOULDN'T UNDERSTAND, WOULDN'T UNDERSTAND. HOW COULD YOU SAY THAT? YOU UNDERSTAND NOTHING ABOUT THIS WAR, NOTHING. YOU WON'T LET IT INTERRUPT YOUR PETTY LIVES. YOU WON'T TRY TO UNDERSTAND." Now it was my turn to stand, and I left the room.

"This has nothing to do with the war," said my father.

I turned back. "It has everything to do with the war, and that is one other thing you don't understand. Life has changed. Everything has changed." And with that, I did leave the room.

They continued to sit there, and from elsewhere in the house I listened to see what sounds came, but I heard nothing. I was harsh, because they did understand that everything had changed. That was why they were so worried about my father's work being still there after the war.

The house was small. The toilet was attached to the ground floor but still outside, beyond the scullery kitchen, in a small outhouse. There was a bathroom upstairs. It should have been a third bedroom, but my parents had, with a lot of excitement, created a bathroom from it just before the war. The one in Cello's house was similar, very heavy pipes that gurgled and spat a liquid that was sometimes brown. It came through a small gas heater, which you had to light, but then it did give some hot or sometimes very hot water. It was better than heating the water on the coal fire in the scullery.

Coal duty, feeding the kitchen ovens, went along with spud peeling and mucking out the horses when you were on guard duty at the barracks. But men under punishment often were there to do these chores. I would be one of the guard corporals when I got to Bordon, supervising these tasks and reporting to an orderly sergeant. Weekend duties would be the same. There would be a lot of corporals there, but I knew I would pick up duty often. That was how it would be.

How would I get time to see Pearl, even if she did come to England? Where would we meet? She had mentioned the invitation to the house of this lady. We could meet there, but … I wanted more. I wanted lodgings where we could be together. We … I was in love.

You could not move about in our house without alerting others. Creaking stairs and doors and heavy curtain movement always gave away a presence. Smells, sometimes musky, and sounds of coal being shovelled into the stove. Then the smell of porridge in the morning, cabbage in the evening. The muskiness was usually mice. The clutter of front rooms usually hid their presence. But I was used to huge rats, so I cared not.

I was tired from the journey and from the front room. I sank into bed without bothering to listen for my parents. I had my own life, which I was determined to lead.

We had done no planning for my seven days leave. Now I regretted not giving my address to Pearl. Letters sometimes took less than seven days to reach me. Of course, the England postal service was good. I assumed hers might not be as good in Jamaica. Still, a letter arriving to break up my week here would be a welcome prospect.

In the morning, my mother made me breakfast. We hardly said a word. She made a lot of scullery noise and pretended to be busy. I headed out for the library. There was a small one in the town.

I did find poetry books and particularly the *Oxford Book of English Verse*. I could not find *The Anansi Stories*.

I walked into town with the poetry book in my hand. The library was a little way out from the centre. There was a small market and behind it a row of shops. It was not a bustling city place like Woolwich, more like a farmers' market town. Animals were brought to be sold in the centre. The smell of manure came from the stains on the heavy railings that formed the animal pens. They were piled to one side of the street this not being a market day. There were more horse vehicles here than Woolwich, bringing sweat and leather smells that comforted in a way, as they were different from those of the hospital. Men in uniform and traders replaced farmers. I avoided eye contact. I knew a new army world would hit me very soon.

I knew of the public houses and could smell the ale, tobacco and whisky odours, but I passed on to a small dusty bookshop I vaguely remembered. It was up a side street.

The doorbell rang inside, summoning a strange stooping old man from the shop depth. I was grateful for this, as I knew he would not challenge my reasons.

"I am looking for a book called *The Anansi Stories*. It is a Jamaican children's book—"

He held up a slightly bent finger. "I know what it is!" he said.

I was struck silent by surprise. I didn't know how this could be. Perhaps this man was the long-lost grandfather I had never known. He knew me as well as the book. Perhaps he knew about Cello and the other executions. I was sure he knew about cellos.

"Umm oh," I expressed dumbly.

"Let me see if I can lay hands ..." He turned slowly. "The place needs a good—"

Tidy, I wanted to complete his sentence, but that was obviously the way he spoke, so I didn't want to make him feel I was commanding him.

The place was a treasure of books, and the untidiness made it more interesting in a way. Piles of books stood precariously in places that should not have supported them. The shelves also bulged. A small set of steps was used to reach the top shelves. But he didn't need them.

"I think ..." He approached a pile in the corner standing next to the gap that gave access to the back of the shop. He bent over so I could not see him searching through. But he muttered as he did as if greeting friends. "Ah, no, not you ... Don't worry, I haven't forgotten you. Ah yes, perhaps ..." He straightened finally. "I think this is what you ..."

He held a small, very slim, and perhaps rather well-thumbed book. It was far from new. But then there didn't seem to be any new books here. He shuffled back to me. He laid the book on the counter. On the front cover was a large perhaps demonic looking black person. At first, it was not clear whether man or woman. He picked it up again as if lovingly. "An unusual request from a ..."

"Yes, perhaps." I found myself smiling for some reason.

"For a friend no doubt." He finally completed a sentence.

"Yes, a friend. You have many books here."

"Of course ... that is the thing about books. You can never have enough. One book leads to another and then another. It is like the rainforest, endless." He looked up into the cobwebby ceiling. "Perhaps I should call my shop Amazon." He laid the book down again.

"Yes, Amazon," I agreed.

"Well, you will be wanting a ..." He produced a small brown bag.

"Yes, I had better."

"That's sixpence."

I paid and left with some regret.

On the way home I passed the pubs without entering as I had things to take home.

But in the remaining days of my leave, I was drawn by the smell and the desire for rum. I sat and smoked and drank for hours. I even spoke to a Private bound for Bordon also. He told me leave was a bore and a regret. He wished he had never come on leave. In a way, I felt the same. My nervousness grew.

The day before I was to join Bordon a letter caught up with me, forwarded from the hospital. It was from Pearl. I retreated to my room. It was a short and breathless letter, although her handwriting remained as perfect as before.

My dearest Benjamin,

It is great news. I have booked my passage and will be arriving in Southampton six weeks from today.

Oh, I have thanked God and my family, especially them as they have come together to help me find the money for the fare. Now I have to prepare for my journey.

I have written to Pamela Smith to say that I am coming. It is a rather presumptuous of me to instantly take up her invitation, which may not have been made in all seriousness. But I must take my life in my own hands. My dear husband, Damien, was taken out of my hands, so I owe it to him to do something myself and this I believe is what I must do.

Oh, my dear, I am excited, and I hope I can count on your support and indeed on your presence at the dockside to welcome me. Oh, I know you have your war to fight, but God has mercifully spared you a return to the front, so I believe that he would have therefore wanted us to meet. I hope that you will be able to seek time off to meet me. I will need your strength to guide me through the new strange land that is England and London.

I am eager to send this so my dear until we meet.

I remain your loving,

Pearl.

Six weeks from today! What today?

I searched the letter and envelope in a rising panic. Then I realised that she had dated her first letter but hardly any others. I had no idea when six weeks from today was.

The day before I had drunk quite a bit.

I had been paid for a month to cover my leave and the first weeks at Bordon, and I was spending that money. Now I realised with a sudden surge of shame that I would need it when Pearl arrived. Also, I would need to buy some things at Bordon. That money I had, which seemed to weigh well in my pocket, was suddenly very light.

But would she come? When would she come?

I had to answer these questions. A telegram might answer both. If I sent one and she replied, I would know the date and whether she was really serious about it.

Why would she not be serious?

But the drink and the words of my mother and father had worked on my mind, and now I had to force it towards my arrival at Bordon and how that would change my life.

Chapter 22

A Game of Football
✳ ✳ ✳

Bordon is like the border of a foreign country. You pass through the massive gate and change. I felt I needed to brace up and be aware of the tapes on my arm. But perhaps it was the shouts that made me do it. Not directed at me I didn't think! But the parade ground was never far away.

I first went to the orderly room to get my billet sorted out, and then the garrison Sergeant Major's office beckoned. I carried my kit bag and suitcase. I had pulled my soft cap down.

After reporting to the Sergeant Major, I knew my life would get small again. I would be trapped.

I heard stamping of feet on gravel and concrete from boots turned from trench to parade ground by the application of layers and layers of polish. Perhaps they hadn't been to the trenches. Perhaps they were a new type of boot.

More shouts, then one voice. "Get out of my office, you 'orrible little man." A door opened in front of me in the covered corridor. A private appeared and braced himself up, then turned towards me. He marched forward and almost brushed me as he passed as if I weren't there. I might even have moved aside.

I knocked. "Come in, if you must!"

"Corporal Routledge, reporting Sar Major." I went in.

"Do you play football, Corporal?" He hadn't even looked up yet.

"Well, I—"

"If you didn't, you do now. Tomorrow, garrison NCOs playing transport section. You look as though you need some fresh air."

"I'm from hospital, Sar Major."

"As I said, you need some fresh air." He sniffed through his moustache as if fresh air was not to his liking.

"Will I be ... where will I be ...?" I seem to have adopted the habit of the book seller of not completing my sentences.

"Come on, you're a corporal on my training team, man. Spit it out!" He didn't have a hat on, and his hair was plastered down a bit probably from too much hat wearing. But his grey eyes and moustache bristled.

"Yes, training team. What will I be doing, Sar Major?"

He stood and was tall, but not overpowering, and I didn't fear the 'orrible little man' label. He placed his hands in front of him, as it measuring an over-large boot. "We are building an army. We are the builders. But sometimes my builders get sent over there as well. I'm short, Corporal. So I really need you. You are going to take over number one platoon, Alpha Company. You are going to be in the top spot, my number one corporal." He sat down, slump-like. Then looked up sharply. "How's your marksmanship."

"I shot three Germans left-handed before I got injured."

He brightened. "A lefty eh. You'll be good for them." He consulted a chart." They've got range tomorrow morning, then infantry tactics. You have seen the new platoon tactics manual, I hope."

I nodded.

"Good, you need to know it inside out. The billet is ... hut 22. You better get over and introduce yourself, bedding store first. You will just make it." He looked up at the clock behind me.

"Sar Major, I need to send a telegram," I blurted.

He looked up. I could hear shuffling outside. It would be part of the evening guard duty under an orderly sergeant. "Family matters, is it?" His voice was actually soft. But it still filled the entire space of his office and somehow resonated on the worn wood floor and the brick walls. The papers lay quietly on the desk as if in a sort of quivering manner.

I nodded again.

"Mailroom ... but it's next to the RSM's office, so be careful. They will accept telegrams."

"Thanks, sir."

He looked at me. "Fourteen hundred sharp, main football pitch. We need to win … with no injuries. Someone got kicked to death in Colchester last week."

I didn't move. *"Kicked to death, God."*

"Yes, they will have an inquiry about it of course. A court-martial might follow, but I doubt it. Now, Corporal, work to do!"

I left the office somehow feeling I had a friend.

Reveille was oh six hundred. I had to get every soldier outside in fifteen minutes for a brief inspection before breakfast. There were thirty of them, fifteen on each side of the hut. My little room was at the end. They were outside before me, "Corp"-ing me as they passed.

"Ben Routledge," I said as they lined up and looked my way.

"Yes, we know, Corp."

"Oh, you know." I looked around. Men were tumbling out of other huts. "Washrooms?" I enquired of the small smiling speaker.

"Can we get grub first?"

"Okay … cookhouse?" But they had gone, running wildly. Some huts were still undergoing inspections.

The last one shouted over his shoulder. "This way, Corp."

So I ran too, not even thinking of my bag of shit, which needed emptying.

Everything was a race, to be at the front of the line, to be ready. To get through whatever you had to do so that you could lounge around on the grass, smoke, and watch others while swaping cards or dirty jokes. But there was no lounging around in the morning. Breakfasted, shaved, bed space squared away, and then out for proper inspection, kitted, and rifle ready before oh seven-thirty was the race.

I had not drawn a rifle from the armoury.

The platoon sergeants and officers approached from their respective messes in a huddle and separated, separated again until you identified the pair approaching. The sergeant was ahead, and the officer hung back a little to allow reports to be made.

"All present and correct, Sarg," I announced.

"Fall in," he replied without a flicker of attention to my newness.

He then marched forward to meet the officer, halted in front of him, and saluted. "Number one platoon present and correct, *sir*."

The officer raised his cane instead of his hand to the peak of his cap. "Very well. Thank you."

He approached me. "Good morning. A replacement corporal, very good. Ready to put them through their paces, I hope!"

"As best as I can, sir," I responded.

"Good, good. Well, follow me round then." He inspected closely, perhaps to impress or test me. "Why is this man's tunic not straight?" he asked me instead of addressing the man.

"Cleaning duties, sir. He had to join us quickly. Straighten yourself up then," I said to the man. I didn't give the officer a chance to hand out a rebuke himself. I took responsibility.

And so I made myself a little popular. I was one of them, but a guide and a mentor as well. That became clear when they lay on the range to shoot. They were working up for their final marksmanship test, which included firing from different positions, a walk and run down from five hundred to one hundred yards and a one minute, sixty rounds rapid fire exercise. You were expected to achieve at least sixty rounds on the kill or disable zone of the target, out of one hundred and twenty rounds fired in all.

I watched at first, then walked with the ones who seemed to be having the most difficulty and lay down with them, encouraging their breathing and the rhythm of their shooting.

During a break, I told my men about my injury and how it had come about. How I shot three German soldiers. They were fascinated by my lefty nature, and I showed how I used the left hand as the vice to hold the rifle still while doing the bolt with my right, then cocking my head further over to the left so that I wouldn't get an ejected cartridge case in my face. I was their friend.

"Corporal Routledge, you seem very familiar with your charges." I was taken aside immediately for a word from the platoon commander.

"I just want them to be confident, sir. That way they will learn and that way they will be better when they arrive in France." This came out automatically, without thinking.

"Quite so. Well, make sure you maintain discipline as well. Rely on you for that as well, you know."

"Of course, sir."

But he couldn't help but notice that they reacted with urgency to the training. There was no sluggishness about them as with soldiers who have no desire to be trained.

After a break, we left the range for a tactics lesson. The sergeant thought he would catch me out and asked me to be in charge of the lesson, with him and the officer as part of the students, which they were. After training, they would all go France. I would stay and wait for the next platoon. I was not fully prepared but had found things in the manual that would help me.

I stood in front of them on a small bank that led up to the range where the next platoon was already into their shooting practice. "When you go to France, things are going to be different," I started.

"Yeah, we're gonna win."

"Yes, you are, but how you going to win?" I immediately turned the question around.

They looked blank. "You might have tanks in support in your attack. How you gonna use 'em?"

They still looked blank.

"Turn around, everybody," I said.

In front of them now was an area of scrubland and some clumps of trees, running back towards our huts. This was our training ground.

"See that scrub there. That's about two hundred yards, isn't it?"

No reply.

"Well, you need to able to estimate distance. We can go over that tomorrow. But say it is. Say that's where the Boche wire is—and of course, it hasn't been broken by the bombardment. How you gonna break it?"

Immediately someone piped up, "With the tanks, Corp."

"Yes exactly. They can be good for that. So you will follow them up. They will lead across the open ground taking out any machine guns or obstacles on the way. Then you will assault through your objective."

"How, Corp?"

"We'll go through that now. Anyone heard of suppressive fire?"

Some had. "Good, let's walk and talk through our assault then. Then, sir, if you don't mind, you can lead them through the next one."

We walked through the new tactics of sections positioning themselves to put down suppressive fire, to cover the other section moving, as per the new manual, with one section acting as bombardier section. I told them they had two Lewis guns with the lead sections. The lieutenant and sergeant surprised me by taking a full and serious part in the training. We walked up and down the space of rough grass, gorse, and bushes. They called out spacing and looked for places to put the Lewis guns, which they didn't have. But they believed they might do.

Finally, the cookhouse beckoned, and we halted and walked back. The lieutenant talked to me. He had respect in his voice asking me about my experiences. I didn't go into a lot of detail. I needed to do two things urgently. One involved a lavatory, of which there weren't very many that were accessible when you were out training.

"Where's the post office," I asked the man in the cookhouse queue in front of me.

"End of the huts then back down into the barracks, first building on end of E block. I'll show you when we get back."

We walked back to the huts after bolting our food down to get ready for the extended afternoon of physical activity.

"We gonna skive off the assault course and come and watch you playing footie," said one casually.

"How did you know I was playing?"

"Word gets around 'ere, Corp," he replied.

I wasn't sure whether to be reassured of this or not. But I had to get to the post office. So I thanked my messenger and headed towards it as soon as I could. I went straight there avoiding eyes, except for salutes thrown up to officers passing. You were supposed to make eye contact then. Not to do so was even viewed as insolent. But then to do so with the wrong expression was also insolence. But these officers did not have the look of judgement in their eyes.

I tried to sneak into the post office recalling that the RSM's office was next door.

A long table greeted me with three or four "posties", working on piles of letters. Sacks hung on hooks behind where letters were deposited, labels were plastered to the walls above them, A COY, B COY, etc. I looked along and noticed GAR COY. That would be Garrison Company, of which I was a part, although I was living with A COY. I would need to take this all into consideration when waiting for letters from Pearl.

"I would like to send a telegram." The place smelt strongly of stale tobacco. We had banned smoking in the hut because of the smell and the fire risk.

The uniformed boy did not blink but pulled out a form. "Sixpence for nine words, a penny for each extra word. Address at the top here." He indicated.

"Can I send it to Jamaica?"

"*Jamaica!*" he exclaimed.

"Yes." I was sweating now.

"No idea how long it'll take, but do it anyway."

YOUR LETTER DID NOT SAY DATE OF ARRIVAL STOP, PLEASE CONFIRM STOP

One word over. Seven pence. I paid, after putting my name and address on the bottom of the form. He looked it over and read it. Nothing was private about a telegram.

I left the office still sweating. I had a strange feeling as I marched back to the hut. Was this the beginning or end for Pearl and me?

I used my PT kit and army boots for the football. I felt sick as I half ran to the pitch, hoping my bag would not just explode out of my shorts. I joined the ones wearing red shirts at the side of the pitch. "Ahhh, you the new Corp?"

"Yes."

"Defender, midfield or up front?"

"Not up front."

"Centre-back then, right or left foot?"

I hesitated. "Left."

"Oh, we need you then. Right, everybody run around the pitch once, then join me in the middle. We've got ten minutes for a kick about till kick off." He was a sergeant from the officers' mess apparently. They needed a sergeant in the officers' mess to keep the batmen in order.

As I ran around, I caught sight of the Sergeant Major and some of my platoon hovering, shirking their training but wanting to see me play. I was nervous about that.

We lined out and then kicked off. My team took the ball forward straight away with one little man who I noticed had a pair of real football boots. He must have been our star player. I relaxed just a little. But he got tackled, and the ball started coming back towards the halfway line. Tackles were going in on men with no attempt to get the ball.

Somebody passed it back, and I found it at my feet. I moved left, taking it with my favoured left foot but almost immediately got hit, and the ball spun out for a throw-in.

The game was going too fast for my poor state of fitness. It came to me again, and I tried to take it on further, but this time the hit took me and the ball out of play. As I stood up, I noticed a familiar and dreaded smell. Then I felt my bag sagging under the waist belt of my shorts. Suddenly the tube, instead of going into my stomach was flapping against my leg. I stopped and looked down.

"Your throw, Corp." People were looking at me and waiting.

"Ref, please, I need some time off the pitch. I … I need a bandage or two."

"Play on," said the ref, ignoring me.

I took myself off and was soon surrounded by my platoon. "I need a bandage," I said from my position sitting on the ground.

"Sickbay, quick lad, bandages." It was the Sergeant Major's voice directing one young soldier. He ran.

I tried to keep myself together.

"From your injury, is it, Corp?"

"Yes, I got this fucking bag and its come unstuck."

"Don't worry. We'll sort you out."

They bandaged me up to keep the shit contained. I would go to the sick bay later. Finishing the game was the important thing.

I did finish it. We won.

Chapter 23

A Flashback and a Photograph
✳ ✳ ✳

I became responsible for the timetabling of my platoon against a training programme written to prepare men for what lay in store for them in France. The range, the different weapons, such as grenades, handheld mortars, the Lewis gun, which all soldiers should be capable of operating. These weapons and the tactics to use them on the move were part of the new training required by the 1917 manual. The tactical movement of platoons across open country and through close country or buildings was constantly hammered home.

The new Fourth Army would be doing all this and working with tanks, although many men scoffed at the possibility of ever seeing one close by. And of course, they broke down very easily.

Of the parade ground there was less sight. The range and the field training area was the new parade ground.

After a brief stay in the sick bay to rectify my bag problems, I was back on the range. My platoon was getting near the end of their training. I would get another platoon once these had gone, to start again from the beginning. My great fear was that I would lose these men, these good men, before Pearl came. The days went by without a reply to my telegram.

Most of the work was now done by the lieutenant and his sergeant, including orders on the range. My job was to hold things together and make sure everything was in place for them to do their training.

I stood at the back of the firing point looking out towards the cardboard targets one hundred yards away. They were shooting by sections from the standing position under the orders of the lieutenant.

"Ready, aim, fire!" Shots rang out.

Suddenly I was back in that little grim farm square in France. In front of me, at about twenty yards, not one hundred, was Cello. They had not tied him to a stake or blindfolded him. He stood there calmly. And even after the first burst of shots, he still stood there so clearly.

I wanted to run forward. "No!" I screamed. Then I did run forward, through the men standing shooting, towards Cello.

"Cease firing!" the lieutenant screamed out.

I dropped to the ground in front of the firing detail. It was hard, stony ground, where bullets flew up with small stones and dust when struck. Sometimes they ricocheted into the air with a fizz, for which there would be a rebuke as it meant men were firing too low. But now there was only silence. Painfully I lifted my head and stared down the range. All I could see were the butts banked up high with a row of cardboard targets on top of them like accusers, Cello's accusers. I searched for signs of him. Had he gone to ground as well or been hit? Where was he? My head sank. Then realisation began to dawn.

"Got ourselves a death wish, have we, Corporal Routledge?" The voice was distinctive. The Sergeant Major had chosen that morning to visit the ranges and had been standing behind the platoon, unseen by most people.

"No, Sergeant Major," I heard myself saying.

"Good, coz I don't want to do the paperwork involved with you getting shot in the line of duty, of you having an unfortunate accident."

Unfortunate accident. Why had he chosen these words? "Well, I … I thought I saw someone in front of the firers, Sar Major. I wanted to warn him."

"I see," he said like a doctor looking into my intestines.

Then a member of the firing detail piped up from behind, "'E was demonstrating a moving target to us, Sar Major." The other members of the section laughed nervously.

"Well, your shooting wasn't very good, then, was it? Obviously, they need extra range work, Corporal."

"We took pity on 'im." There was more laughter at this other comment.

"You are doing quite well, Mr Routledge, aren't you? A little accident on the football pitch, now nearly got shot on the range, and you haven't been here, what, two weeks yet?"

"I'll try to stay alive, Sar Major," I replied.

"Yes, you better had. I need you to be alive. This is not France."

"Thank you." Now I was sitting up and looking back at the firing section, which had grounded their rifles. I was crying, but being in the mood for other emotion, another of them started laughing, and I found myself doing the same.

"Perhaps we should have a few words in my office when you have some spare moments."

"Yes, Sar Major."

"But for now, carry on, men. NEXT FIRING DETAIL."

And on we went.

I was exhausted that evening and lay on my bunk after the supper meal. There was a knock on the door. The partition did not go up the ceiling, so I heard every word and movement from outside, but still, the knock was done, and I didn't know who was there as he had not announced himself over the top of the door.

"Come in."

"Evening, Corp. You got a minute?"

"Yes, Ralph. Come in." I was beginning to get to know them all by their first names. It seemed to me the right thing to do. All officers and NCOs used different nicknames or swear words or other forms of down-talking address to privates and recruits. A second name delivered in a certain tone that was the norm could also imply a variety of meaning worse than a swear word. As for me, they needed a friendly voice talking at their level.

I needed a friendly voice as well.

"Got someut you may be interested in."

"Oh, yes."

He stood there for a moment before sitting on the one wooden chair I had, my piece of posh furniture. There was also a wooden locker for my uniform. The kit lay on the floor. He was short and slim. Recruits generally were. I remember a nurse once commenting on the quality of manhood among soldiers, mentioned that many had fallen in chests and skinny legs. I had become somewhat like that. Ralph though had a wide smile and a very willing nature, as well as a sharp wit. He had a dirty brown envelope, out of which he pulled a newspaper cutting with a picture.

He spoke with a Worcestershire accent sucking in his cheeks over his Rs, which he said like they were oars. "Was you in this, Corp?" It was the photograph of the battalion taken as they were going up to Arras before the whole Cello thing.

"Yes." I scanned it eagerly, but the faces were blurred. "I was way in the middle, not out in front or nothing. That was when our old RSM was killed. He organised the photo then just stood there as we marched past, looking so proud. Then a shell took him out right there where we had been. Looks very smiley and jolly though doesn't it."

"Yes, it does."

"Rubbish, even then we were desperate and exhausted. The good stuff they did at Vimy was all turned back to stalemate." I passed the picture back to him. "Where did you get it?"

"Been saving it up ever since it first came out in paper ... this time it gonna be different, Corp, ain't it?"

I sighed, which perhaps I should not have done.

"Yes, it is, Corp. You guys were the trialists. You set it up last year, now we gonna finish everything. I know about this and the other false starts. Going right back to Gheluvelt, which left a bitter taste ... and the eight men who were executed. I know about them ... and the bloke what got the VC and was due to come home on leave to collect his gong from the king and the whole town were waiting for him. But he didn't come home coz he'd been killed ... But we gonna put all that right. We ... you have shown us how to conquer fear as well."

"*Me!* How."

"You have, by your confidence and kind of ... humility."

"Humility! I don't know about that. But how do you know all this, Ralph?"

"My brother. He told me when he was home on leave a couple of times."

I daren't ask him whether his brother was still alive. "You said about the eight men executed did you know there was another, my friend. I saw him today on the range—that's why I did that."

"No, I didn't know."

"He was a reinforcement, not Worcesters—that's probably why."

"What happened?"

"It was an injustice. Maybe I will tell all of you. But not right now."

"I think all of them were injustices, but that's the point about war, ain't it? Everything is an injustice."

I looked at him anew. "Do you play the cello, Ralph?" I suddenly asked stupidly.

He laughed. "*Cello*, what is it, some musical instrument? No, Corp … I mean, Ben, never even seen one."

We both laughed.

He looked on the bed where my book of the *Anansi Stories* was lying. "What's this?"

"A book of stories," I said.

"Yeah, kiddies stories, is it?" He was looking at me slightly strangely.

"Yes, they are mostly about a spider that has human characteristics and a kind of naughty streak in his character."

He stared at me. "Yes, Corp, very good bedtime reading for you."

We laughed again.

"It's my lady friend, her favourite childhood book, and I thought I would read it to get to know her better." I said it so frankly and simply, without any thought or embarrassment.

His face, which was freckled with bright ginger hair above it, broke open with a big smile. "Great idea, Corp."

I felt a heady power to impart my secret. "She's a coloured woman."

His expression did not change. "Corp, you are a strange one. But I envy you."

"Do you?"

"Yes, of course."

"Don't you want to know how I met her? Give you another string to your endless knowledge about regimental history."

"Course. Go on, then."

I felt that the whole hut would be outside the door listening. But I told Ralph anyway about Midnight and how he had rescued me and how I had written to Pearl afterwards.

He sat back at the end and looked me. "Corp, you have done well. I wish you good fortune, you and your lady friend."

We looked at each other and laughed. Tears were about to come as well. A corporal would never have cried before this war, but I had already done it in front of them when I had the flashback of Cello on the range. He made a move to go. I knew that my story would be all around the hut before morning. But I wanted to hear his secret first. "And your brother?"

He was standing. "He is no longer with … us."

I didn't say anything. Words, as when I was with Cello's parents, are totally inadequate sometimes. I nodded. The looks of understanding we gave each other were enough.

Then he brightened. "But I have a younger brother and sister, and they are too young to get into this war."

"Look after them," I said. As he held the brown envelope in his hand, I added, "And look after that photograph."

As he left, I missed him straight away but looked forward to the next day's training with all of them. I went outside for a smoke in the fading light of evening.

Chapter 24

My Instructions Arrive

✳ ✳ ✳

Some of the things Ralph told me about what had happened while I was lying in the hospital gave me a sort of dragging regret about what I had missed. The regiment is a whole world, and some soldiers can be part of it like Ralph. Others take no part in regimental life. They are disciplined along unwillingly, like children on the periphery of a game. Regimental life was a sort of game, in which support needed to be given at football matches to your battalion. Friends in different battalions often exchanged letters. Some soldiers actually listened during lectures about regimental tradition. Ralph probably took notes.

It was different when you were in battle. Formations of brigades, divisions, and at the end the whole army did not always take account of regiments. You might have two battalions from the same regiment in one brigade, but there would be other battalions as well from a very different part of the country. The regiment tried to be a family—or, as I had called it in my interview with the company commander in the hospital, a tribe. But mostly those family benefits came when you were on home duty or training.

Our regiment had swelled to fourteen battalions during the war from four at the start and two militia battalions. It was a man-eating machine, constantly in need of reinforcement. But these were not always forthcoming, although now the depot seemed to be full to bursting. I dreaded the day Ralph and the other platoon members were shipped to France, as they would be.

I read the *Anansi Stories* by a weak light that served the whole hut. I marvelled at the language of the stories, which seemed like a kind of Jamaican slang, I supposed. My mother despised accents, as she regarded them as a mark of the wrong class. But I assumed from Pearl's letters that she would have a very posh accent. However, she still liked the slang of the Anansi stories. This turned the whole class structure upside down. The writer who had written the stories must have loved the slang as well to have written it. But since Midnight himself seemed a man not classed with an accent, I assumed Pearl would be the same.

I smiled at this. How proud I would be if I ever came to introduce Pearl to my parents and they found her to have the manners and voice of someone they themselves aspired to be? Even if she spoke with the accent of the stories, I could not perceive her as of a lower class.

Ralph and the whole platoon greeted me the morning after our conversation, as they did each morning. There was some sniggering. Soldiers are never short of a snigger. But it did not seem to be filled with scorn, at least not when directed at me.

They wanted stories.

We smoked outside the hut. There was no rum to hand around. They spoke of it and moaned over the price. Some had been to a pub in the town where the manager had been summoned and threatened to report them for being AWOL. But actually, they were not. Civilians were always quick to accuse soldiers of some misdemeanour, thinking themselves to have some power over them.

Platoons were allowed one evening out during the last few weeks of their training. Then they were allowed a day or two of leave before going to France. Embarkation leave was a privilege but also a kind of curse, as many men got depressed by contact with their mothers and fathers. Some bragged of lovers and wives, but in reality few had them.

So they envied me. Although many did have pen lady friends, who wrote to them and wished them well and spoke of home and family life, these pen pals were usually the butt of derision. Men thought they were old maids or ugly spinsters or even men seeking a queer friendship. Photographs of these "pals" seemed hard to come by.

My relationship was more than one at the end of a pen. Although as I waited for a reply to my telegram, it was difficult to believe that this was so. Days spread into a week, then two. I must have looked anxious as men enquired about me? "How are you going, Corp. How's the future misses, Routledge?" This stunned me, but the others in earshot laughed. Family, of whatever nature was a gift which for so many, like Ralph, had been torn apart.

They became a team. This was a bit sad as they wouldn't stay as one. On arrival at the Corps staging post they might be split, depending on the regimental needs. Two battalions were in this division or that one. Officers were different and would be allocated to a battalion. There were always vacancies. They might be lucky and stay together until they reached the divisional logistics area. Then they would become reinforcements.

Their training progressed. Grenade throwing was always good for a laugh or two. Some young recruits might drop them at the feet of instructors and NCOs before the thrower himself would dive for cover. But this platoon seemed more at ease with itself and its fate. I knew they would make good soldiers. They already were, some returning from courses and injury or late joiners. On or two had been to military detention centres from which they had been rehabilitated back into the normal service.

To them, Cello's story, as I unfolded it, was not unusual or a surprise. They were amused at the song though. "How did it go, Corp. Go on sing it for us!"

"I can't."

"So after that they just did it, they shot him?"

"Yes."

"Couldn't do it after singing with him," said one, and silence fell among us, except for the sounds of the range and the parade ground. They seemed far off.

Then someone lifted the bolt on his Lee Enfield and yanked it back with a well-oiled rattle. No magazine was on and no round inside, of course. We were lounging outside the hut on the grass, cleaning rifles and preparing for an afternoon on the range.

A soldier's life can change on a moment in a casual way. At that moment a recruit from another hut approached us and suddenly dropped an envelope beside me. "Postie asked me to give you this, Corp. Arrived this morning."

This was plain for all to see. I picked it up and looked around in a kind of triumphant way. I knew it was from Pearl, but a letter, not a telegram.

The reaction of the platoon was the same as my fellow patients in the hospital, but it was also totally different. They descended on me like kids. "Give it here, Corp. We want to read it."

But I slipped it between my tunic buttons and against my white vest before they could lay hands on me. "No, you bastards. Time to fall in. Otherwise, you'll all be joining me on duty this evening."

It was sod's law that I was one of the guard corporals that night, which meant sleeping in the guardroom. But perhaps I would be able to read the letter in peace, I reasoned, because in the hut I probably wouldn't have any of that.

The afternoon proceeded smoothly without me trying to get in front of rifles again.

We had our supper meal, and I headed for my duties at the guardroom.

First I had to take over the guardroom from the day duty corporal. I inspected the two ranks of the night guard outside the guardroom, twenty men in all, detailed the men under punishment to their duties in the cookhouse, and then waited for the orderly sergeant. He again inspected and then waited for the orderly officer. Normally the orderly officer did not inspect the guard, as he would want to get back to the bar in the officers' mess. He had certain duties during the evening and would need to do rounds at least twice during the night, ensuring the barracks sentries and wandering patrols were doing their duties before returning to his bed.

I was the guardroom supervisor, so I wouldn't get much sleep.

But I couldn't wait any longer, so I hastily left the guardroom under the charge of a senior storeman who I knew to be reliable before sneaking into the little bunk space at the back of the guardroom.

My dearest Benjamin,

I write in haste as I prepare to board my ship. I cannot believe that in just ten days I shall be in England.

My dear, I hope you have not forgotten me as I have waited in vain for a letter from you. I know you are busy with your new job and it is probably taxing for you, but please try to be there to meet me, particularly as I arrive in Southampton and I will then have to get to London. This will be a first boat trip for me but also a first train trip as we journey from Southampton to London.

I have a letter from Pamela informing me of her address and saying she is looking forward to my arrival. So everything would seem to be in place apart from word from you. However, I have confidence in you, and I know you will do your best for me.

Remember, it is the 10 May at around midday that we dock and the ship is the SS MONTEVIDEO.

In loving anticipation

Pearl.

I had a date, but it was in three days' time. My heart dropped. But by some freak of chance, the whole platoon was approaching the end of their training and was due a two-day leave pass this weekend.

Chapter 25

I Am Breathless
✳ ✳ ✳

The parade ground was overlooked by a clock tower whose clock sounded like a high-pitched toy. It did not resound with the confidence of a church bell. This was toy town, and we were tin soldiers. I stood on parade the day after receiving Pearl's letter. The platoon was getting ready for its passing out. It was getting ready to be shipped to France. This was a kind of rehearsal for that.

I was the right marker of the platoon. As I stretched my eyes to the left, I caught the front rank, their polished boots and peak caps pointing forward, all in line ready for inspection. The garrison colonel always inspected the senior platoon, the one almost ready to go out to join the war. Before he did so, the RSM took over the parade. I don't know how many platoons there were on parade that day. I only knew that the colonel would inspect my platoon, and if there was anything, anything at all wrong, our final weekend would be cancelled and my hope, my only hope, of meeting Pearl would be dashed to pieces.

The clock struck nine as the RSM came to attention. The toy clock, we the toy soldiers stood rigidly to attention. Each of us was a lonely sentry, with lonely thoughts. We had on the uniform of the army, badges of the regiment, the equipment of war, but our thoughts were not visible, our backgrounds were not visible, whether we were cello players or draughtsmen or farm hand was not known.

I sweated.

The RSM surveyed the ranks. His head went this way and that. Then it stopped, and he looked directly at us. "Number five, the rear rank of number one platoon Alpha Company, GET YOUR CAP ON STRAIGHT. DO YOU THINK YOU ARE A COAL MINER WITH HIS CAP ON THE BACK OF HIS HEAD READY TO CARRY A SACK OF COAL?" He paused … to draw breath. His words had blasted out across the parade ground.

He continued. "CORPORAL, SORT OUT YOUR MEN NOW!"

"VERY GOOD, SIR!" I heard myself shout. I took one pace forward and turned right. I doubled into the gap between the middle and rear ranks and stopped at number five. "Ground arms … now sort out yur cap, for gawd's sake." I didn't use his first name though I knew it.

He pulled it down a shade, then bent and took up his rifle again.

The whole parade was waiting. I doubled back to my position and took it up smartly.

The RSM paused momentarily. NCOs knew this was a ritual, designed to impress. He probably had seen the cap, but sometimes he would refer to some soldier's boots, or the tightness of his rifle sling, leaving people to wonder how on earth he could see that. Often he could not.

"LOOK UP EVERYWHERE AND STAND STILL."

He turned about and began to march towards the saluting dais, a raised wooden platform on which stood some officers. The adjutant, a tall figure in breeches and carrying an extra long cane, moved down from the dais. Salutes took place. Words were spoken. In turn, the adjutant surveyed us. He said nothing and then he turned. The garrison colonel, a slightly ponderous officer, shuffled to the centre of the dais and received the adjutant's report. He then took the two steps down and proceeded in a meandering manner towards us.

My heart was pounding.

"Name?" enquired the colonel to me.

"Routledge, sir."

"Are these men ready for what lies ahead?"

"I believe so, sir."

The inspection started. The colonel was followed by the adjutant, the RSM, the platoon commander, who had fallen in behind the adjutant as they approached from the dais, and the sergeant, who had been in his parade position at the rear of the platoon. All of them could have picked on a soldier for something wrong with his appearance.

But the colonel was more interested in talking to the men. "Are you confident in your use of the Lewis gun?"

"How would you expect the platoon to be split up in an attack across open ground?"

"What do you understand by the expression 'creeping barrage'?"

He took a long time and talked quite a bit. I was proud of the way the men answered. It gave us what we wanted—a weekend off.

It was the strangest twist of fate that this was also the weekend that Pearl was to arrive. I knew that if I could not get leave, I would go AWOL.

We marched off, and I headed for the Sergeant Major's office.

"Well, Mister Routledge survived the inspection, did we?"

"Yes, quite well, Sar Major."

"Good, well, I've got the platoon leave requests, but I haven't got yours. Fancy a bit of extra duty, do we?"

"No, Sar Major ... I was waiting for my plans to be ... I do need a two-day pass and a warrant for travel to Southampton and then to London."

"One warrant and one destination. You know that, Corporal, don't you?"

"Yes, I do."

"So which is it to be, Southampton or London?"

"Umm, Southampton then." I knew I had to go there, so it was the obvious choice. But I would have to pay for the train to go to London with Pearl.

"You are a right headache. Very well, platoon leave passes and warrants will all be issued tomorrow, along with ... pay. Zero eight hundred on Saturday is the start time. Get the platoon to my office after the last period tomorrow."

"Very well." I paused. "You said I should come and have a chat after the incident on the range Sar Major ... do you?"

"Water under the bridge old, son, isn't it?"

"Yes, I think it is."

I returned to the hut thinking about the "old son" that he addressed me as. I slept wonderfully well that night.

On the next day, there was an atmosphere of end of term about the platoon. They did not go to the range or the parade ground. They had physical training and a minor tactics run through the woods behind the huts where obstacles had been dug into the mud and built into banks and enemy trenches dug. Most of the obstacles consisted of sandbags and wire. Trenches had been riveted with corrugated iron and wooden posts. They had to move through the area as if they were attacking it, using suppressive fire sections and bombardier men to creep up close the trenches and throw grenades in. These were not live grenades. The ammunition used was blank. They had done this many times before. Now they needed a new challenge. The following week, the final short week would be spent combining with other platoons to produce a company manoeuvre.

They had to clean up afterwards and have their meal and make themselves presentable for the sergeant major's pay and leave parade. Pay was, of course, the most exciting thing of everything, and there was endless talk about what they would do.

The hut was bustling with activity. "What about you, Corp? Pity the young lady's not over here, ain't it?"

I pondered whether to tell them my news. The next week they would plague me with demands for detail so I thought I should tell them. "Well, she is coming to England, actually, this weekend."

They were aghast. "You lucky bastard. How they hell did you pull that off?"

"Well, it wasn't me it was her. You know women can take matters into their own hands now. The suffragettes are leading women to do all kinds of stuff."

"Not right for women, says I," piped up one voice from a bed halfway down the hut. "*Votes for women!*"

"Yeah, what they voting for?"

"Well, bigger breasts, I'd say."

"Less underclothes. Have you ever tried getting a girl's bloomers off when she's struggling a bit?"

"Let 'em do it while you sit and have a smoke."

I interrupted. "Pay parade, twenty minutes. Make it snappy, men."

"Shit, Corp, we are on it."

"You better had be."

The Sergeant Major liked to give one of his little pep talks at this time. It happened every week as one platoon passed for duty. We stood in a hollow square formation outside his office. "At ease, gentlemen, please." That really impressed the lads, to be called gentlemen, and they murmured approval. He cleared his throat then spoke slowly and clearly. "Gheluvelt, Gallipoli, Beaumont Hamel, Arras. You know these names. Memories of them cause some bitterness. Bitterness at our losses. At our unredeemed losses. Often the result of a battle was a withdrawal and a giving back of territory we had fought and died over. In the earth of some of those places remains the blood of men who went through these gates and did what you have done. They gave their blood unselfishly. They are waiting patiently for you. Because, like in a game of football, there can always be a rematch, and the result can be different.

"You will make the result different. This time there will be no giving back, no stalemate. There will be an end, once and for all. You will be part of that. I wish every one of you the best of good fortune. I ... we (he looked at me) will be with you in spirit. That is the way of a regiment, one spirit ...

"And talking of spirits I have here a free nip for you all. Rum is not easy to come by here, but we have our ways. Now, line up for your pay and then straight into the office one at a time, where you will get your ration. Down in one as always, eh."

The cheers that greeted this oration were unrestrained. They lined up. I was last. The door of the office was opened, revealing a desk on which the brown envelopes of money were arranged. In they filed called in alphabetical order.

Heady but happy we all drifted back to the hut. My heart was so greatly cheered and swelled that I almost wondered whether I should forget Pearl and volunteer for weekend duty after all. How would she find me?

I smiled to myself. Every evening outside the gates some women gathered to check if men had been released on leave. Tomorrow some would be there. Some said they were whores; some undoubtedly were. I felt that Pearl, who of course had my address, would find her way here. Then I would be the nagged husband, the henpecked. Word would be around that Routledge's "black whore" was after him. Perhaps she had his baby. Yes, that would get around.

I could not have that. I was not a coward anymore. The dead Cello, the dead Midnight, and now this woman had cured my cowardice. It was time for me to stand up.

I slept fitfully.

I was awoken by a knock on the outside door of the hut. It had been light a long time. During training, we would have been out and at it. Some men had already left. My train would be … when I knew not. I cursed at the time and my lack of forethought. I had to get to the station. Would I get there in time?

Outside was a telegram boy who worked in the garrison post office. "Corporal Routledge?"

"Yes." I could not even draw breath.

"Telegram, sir."

"Thank you."

I didn't go back into the hut to face men going about their leave routine. I went around the side of the hut and crouched on the ground away from any of the windows. My hands trembled.

It was sent from the ship.

ARRIVAL PORT NOW TILBURY 1400 STOP

No more words. They would have cost too much.

She probably didn't know that Tilbury was near London. But how …

Could I change my warrant? Shit, the Sergeant Major had told us he was also away, so there were to be no last-minute requests. We should just go on leave and enjoy ourselves.

Perhaps I could change my warrant at the station. The station staff might allow that. How would I have sufficient money if I didn't do that? The train fare to Tilbury alone would drain it. I knew that Tilbury was a large embarkation port, although when first embarking for France I had gone from Felixstowe. So it would be a strange place for me.

I sweated, and my breath would not come. I had to run.

Lorries took men to the station. I caught one. I was breathless beyond my lungs. My heart was bloodless.

Chapter 26

I Am Speechless
✳ ✳ ✳

By the time I got to the station, I had regained some breath, although the thick, smoky atmosphere in the back of the truck made me cough.

At the ticket office queue, I became nervous again. Finally arriving at the dirty window, I asked to change my warrant for Tilbury.

"You got a cheek, ain't ya, son!" The ticket inspector sat so close to the window that I could smell his breath, which did have a slight whisky whiff, through the speaking grill. But then he saw my corporal's stripes and pushed his cap back on his head. He seemed to notice the oak leaf on my 1914–18 war medal, which almost none of the other soldiers shuffling through on leave yet had. "Well, if it's important ... I guess the governor could stretch it a bit."

"Yes, it is important."

"Irregular y'noe ... but just a minute." He hovered a pen over the hand-written warrant then changed the destination. He pegged the warrant on the skewer with the others being careful that the spike went through word Tilbury. Then he looked up at me and winked. I smiled.

"Actually, you be better orf with that coz you gonna git there a might quicker." He consulted his timetables and drew out a sheaf of tickets. "Be ten o'the clark number five." He handed me two tickets, outward and return.

It was my lucky day. I separated from some soldiers I had arrived with and joined others on the bustling platform. More civilians seemed to be heading for London, including ladies in long heavy skirts and hats.

I looked at the ladies especially, perhaps comparing to Pearl. Of course, none were coloured. I remembered Pearl's comment about Pamela Colman Smith. "Some say she is a woman of colour."

It was a short wait, and then, boarding with many others, I headed for the nearest carriage. I squeezed straight into a seat against the window, not having to worry or fuss about getting boxes and bags onto the luggage netting above. I was lucky getting one. Everybody wanted to lose themselves looking out of the window instead of being sandwiched between people who you tried not to look at or converse with.

It had been raining as we arrived at the station and boarded the train, and my uniform began to give off an odour of dampness. The heavy, rough material—a mixture of dark green and brown—got wet and then dry as you wore it for everything, buttoned to the neck with a white vest and braces underneath, no shirt, collar or tie. One change hung in my locker. It could be professionally cleaned or hand washed. Ironing it was a devilish job. In the trenches, no one worried about such things. But when you came to wear it on an outing, you realised that it was not the dress for such an event.

We moved through the English countryside. My fellow passengers were also wet. So I was relieved that they too had an odour. Heavy clothes, pipes, cigars, and other smoking material made the air thick. People bustled in and out of the carriage, bringing distraction. Their class and speech and way of conduct made me think of my appearance. I had been looking at my nails and thinking of my hair and face. I was just another soldier in his uniform. People expected the somewhat earthy, uncut nails, the slicked hair, and of course the moustache, a bit stained around the mouth from smoke going through it.

I had recovered from the several nips of rum of the previous evening. Some of the platoon had declined their portions, so I had taken advantage. I'm sure Pearl would not approve.

I was going to a meeting with a woman. I did not know how it might take place. The ship would arrive. I was convinced of that. But how would I single out Pearl? Probably she would be the only black woman. Excitement began to take hold of me.

We would change at Waterloo and take another train direct to Tilbury.

There would be throngs of soldiers at Tilbury. It was the embarkation port for many going to France; the scene of many goodbyes and the holding back of tears.

But this was a new world. I had shed tears in front of my platoon. Women did shed them on station platforms. But women were not weak, because after shedding tears they became suffragettes and went and threw Molotov cocktails in Downing Street.

I heard the often stated query: "What's the world coming to?" on the train as people tutted at some tiny inconvenience of bureaucracy that made their travelling more difficult. But perhaps they were referring to the cut of the suit of the person sitting next to them.

Ticket inspectors came and went. All tickets in my carriage seemed in order.

As we approached London, I heard something that made my heart drain. "It's all down to the aliens act."

"Well, it'll keep undesirables out of this country, won't it."

Since 1905 there had been laws to govern who came into the country, and during the war, these had been tightened up to stop enemy agents entering. Those disembarking had to have permission to disembark. Some were even refused, having arrived in the country.

Surely Pearl would be fine. She was after all the widow of a man who had fought. But then I remembered her telling me of the lynching in America, which had happened in some cases to men who had fought!

In London, I was hungry and crowded into the platform sandwich bar to get some refreshment. I drank tea, spilling almost all my cup over the table. I eat bread and cheese without butter. "Rations are hitting us hard," said the woman behind the counter when I looked at the butterless bread. I thought about the meals at Cello's house, how small they had been. Probably those parents would be even more desperate now, trying in vain to get some answers from the war office.

A mournful whistle and a hiss of steam announced the arrival on the platform of my train to Tilbury. The station clock showed 1245. "What time do we arrive in Tilbury?" I asked the boarding guard.

"1415, sir," he responded.

This was almost perfect timing. At last I had got something going my way.

My seating was not so lucky this time. A sailor opposite tried to pick a fight with me. "Where's your rifle and pack then, soldier? What sort of a soldier are you?"

"I'm going on leave."

"No one goes on leave to Tilbury. That's where they go *to* leave, to leave this country, to fight! You gonna fight?"

"Already have."

"Oh, so it's over for you, is it?"

"No, it's not over. I do my bit now."

"Ever been to sea?"

"No."

"That's different, facing them Hun U-boats."

I noticed he didn't have any medals.

"Your ship at Tilbury, is it then?" I asked.

"Yeah, stopped to take on stores then back out this evening. We sail into the Atlantic: convoy protection."

"Good luck."

I was in no mood for a fight or argument. I knew they could happen, even on trains. The other people in the carriage seemed to relax.

There was little or no countryside to look at. The train puffed and whistled through industrial brick stacks with great warehouses and yards and the backs of houses. Then came the river Thames tributaries, over which we rattled time and again. Mud banks cradled barges moored down the centre, stuffed with something and topped with great tarpaulins. Ropes stretched from them making webs.

Unceremoniously, brakes screeched towards the end of the line. The time was well after 1400.

"Tilbury docks. All change, please. All change."

The banging of doors began. Everybody upheaved. Possessions came down from the nets including my small case. I glanced at the sailor. He had a small kitbag. He nodded.

The platform was a mass of people. A sign at the end of the platform read: **TO THE DOCKS.** That's where everybody was going. I didn't know what my heart was doing. It was empty of expectation. It was a void in my being. I was borne along. Some great gates opened onto the dock area and our tickets were taken as we crowded through. This was even greater than I had experienced when first embarking for war. But it was geared for war embarkation and freight loading. I could see ships masts and funnels in the near distance as we walked. There was concrete below our feet. Then there were tram lines, then wooden decking. We had come off a passenger train, but alongside a freight train was being unloaded of guns. We were heading for another huge sign: **LINER TERMINAL.**

I had started searching for black people, particularly women. There were some. But they toiled in long white apron-like dresses with goods. I suspected that they were servants. Men strutted with dark suits and voices were everywhere, but you couldn't pick any out. The noise of traction overarched everything, of movement of people and machines.

We passed one, two ships, but not Pearl's, *SS Montevideo*, and then came abreast a great building with a cavernous opening and pillars on either side. A sign stood on high above this portal: **ALIEN REGISTRATION.** I knew this was where she would have to go.

Unlike outside, where machines ruled, voices did here, in a low, constant hubbub. I lost myself for what seemed minutes, wandering, and then began to fear as I got so far from the doorway that I would miss some entrance that Pearl might make.

Then I found her desk. A small flag above a simple desk with steps up to it proclaimed: *SS Montevideo.* I hardly dared to look.

I needn't have looked at all. In front of me, a figure turned as if someone had tapped her on the shoulder. There was a swish of her dress which did not conceal the energy of the limbs beneath it, limbs that had a certainty of purpose. I stood very still, and she said afterwards that was how she knew it was me. I was still.

Well, actually, I couldn't move anyway. And as she slowly approached, I must have looked stupid because I couldn't say anything either.

Chapter 27

I Am in a Different World
✳ ✳ ✳

"Is it Benjamin?" She put out a hand, and I looked at it. There was a line down the top edge of the hand, a dividing line between the smooth brown back of the hand and the almost white palm.

I took the hand, and with my left hand, I removed my cap. I didn't answer the question. A flood was passing over me out of which I couldn't hang onto anything of my previous thoughts about our meeting, our situation, our future. Everything that I considered to say or think was lost in the flood.

She put her head slightly on one side as I just looked. She was probably wondering whether I could actually speak. There were wisps of curly hair around her face, then her dark, long, flicking curls above that. Then a hat: not one that looked like an upside chimney pot which hid the hair but a round one with brim turned up that showed her face and hair. I had registered the hand, but I did not register her face colour, only the eyes and the white teeth.

"I'm sorry," I managed to stammer. "I had meant to meet you off ... as you came off the ship. Is it here?" This was a totally stupid question.

"It's outside," she said and laughed.

I should have laughed. How would the ship be in the shed? But some of the sheds in this huge dockland did have dry docks for ships.

"Have you ... your papers?" I indicated the desk around which people were clamouring.

"All done." She held up a small booklet. "I have my passport, and the landing has been stamped. So I'm now free!" She spoke with a freedom, with a slightly rolling accent. Her confidence and presence completely overwhelmed me. I didn't know what to do next.

"Free?" I continued in my hopelessly ignorant way.

"Free to go."

"Oh ... yes. Well the station is back and outside ... as well."

Then we both did laugh, though it was nervous for me.

"Shall I take your ..." I indicated her case, which was quite small, like mine, which was surprising as she had come far further than me. Then I thought that maybe she was only passing and wouldn't stay. I put my cap back on and took her suitcase. In truth, I was grateful to have something to occupy both hands as I thought she might expect me to hold her hand or want to hold her hand.

She walked free. I looked at her. She was very slightly ahead as we moved towards the great doorway. We passed many people, but I had eyes only for Pearl. Eventually, she said, "Why are you looking at me?"

"Because you are a lady." This was the first good thing I said.

"Thank you very much, Benjamin." She smiled.

Had I been expecting a sort of servant looking girl in a long white apron? Pearl wore a straight brown dress with a long, full skirt ending just above her ankles and a layered blouse, which was also part of the dress, falling to below the waist. This part was pleated and came to her neck.

"And I am just a common soldier."

"No, you are not Benjamin. You are a person: a unique person."

We were outside and moving along the dockside towards the station. I was aware that people were looking at me, us. That did not worry me.

She looked around. "That's my ship over there." She indicated the third one along the dock.

"Ohh, I see ... Shall we go to your friend's house? You got the address?" I was beginning to find my voice, although it was nervous. I was also aware that she had never been to London. I was beginning to feel Pearl's freedom as well. It was the same as Cello had shown me.

"Yes. I have it." We were passing a bench, and she said, "Shall we sit down and look at it?"

We sat quite close. She drew out a letter and looked it through. "She's

183

even given me the nearest station, which is, I think … yes, Charing Cross. She is working as an illustrator with a theatre near there. But the work she says is 'sporadic', so she wants some company." She looked at me. "Would it be appropriate for you to stay there too?"

I felt breathless with her directness. It made my world of army restraint slip away. Stories of weekends in London or anywhere were recounted in wonder. "I have leave until Monday."

She tensed with excitement. "Yes, that's wonderful, Benjamin."

"But how long will you stay with her, your friend?"

"Well, I think we shall have to find out. I could go back. Do you want me to go back … home?"

"Not on Monday, no."

"How far is your barracks?"

"A long train journey."

"Let's not talk of that now. How do we get to Charing Cross?"

"We can get a ticket here." We were nearing the station, passing through the gates. Pearl showed the stamps in her passport. I was aware of the seemingly pitiful amount of money in my uniform pocket. "Do you want me to get your ticket?" I asked.

"Oh no, I have a little money. I know your pay is so small. Damien sent money to me, but it was not much. It was all he had."

I breathed again. We got our tickets. I was able to convert part of my return warrant to go via Charing Cross. "You must be hungry," I blurted as we passed a platform stall selling some pie and mash food.

"Oh, not really. I'm sure Pixie will have something in the house."

"Pixie?"

"Yes, Pamela, my friend. Her name is also Pixie."

I laughed. "Pixie sounds interesting."

"Oh, she is interesting, very interesting lady."

I was nervous. The bustle of trains and strangers does not allow intimateness to begin. We had no foundation for it, and we were going to another stranger's house.

We did not take a taxi because of money, so we walked through streets still in broad daylight. At night no light is turned on because of the threat of Zeppelins. We were close as we walked. "Are you cold?" I asked.

"No, I think the ocean air has made me used to it, Benjamin." She stopped in shadow. I stood in front of her. "We are about to begin a new life. I don't want to start being cold."

I placed the suitcases down and looked straight into her eyes. "I want a new life. I don't have a life now and not much prospect when this war is over. I don't have much to offer you."

"Yes, you do."

"You know I have some after effects of my injury … I can't do all my … I have a bag for my toilet. They call it a colostomy bag." I started to shake a little. I hadn't chosen the moment and place to say it.

"As far as I am concerned, you are a man. You are a good man. I want to know more about you. Let us go along now. We will have plenty of time to talk."

We went in silence having lost the crowd, for a bit, looking in doorways for a number. We found it. Everything was quiet and still.

But after the door opened nothing seemed still anymore, and I was introduced to a new world. "Ahh, my dears, my lovers, come in." A shortish bobbing woman met us. She was enveloped in a dress of considerable proportions. She was pale. We went into the front room, and she closed the door then bustled about upping the gas wicks. There were heavy curtains at the windows preventing daylight entering. "Ahh, let me look at you. What a handsome couple. Let me hug you both."

The closeness and the touching bridged any embarrassment. Afterwards, I realised I had not been hugged like that in uniform before. "Now, I am Pixie, and you are Pearl, and you are Ben." She held our hands one of ours with each of hers.

"Yes," we chorused.

She giggled with a strange girlish expression screwing up her face. "Oh, you must be so tired. Well, well indeed, all the way from Jamaica with your little suitcase—to start a new life. How exciting! You are welcome, my dear. We will be friends, I know we will. And with your handsome soldier, Ben, with his medal and corporal's stripes. Leave your cases a bit. Sit down."

We sat in embroidered chairs, and she reclined on a sort of sofa. I looked around the room. It was impossible to take in everything. There were images on the wall I recognised from the *Anansi Stories*, weird and funny pictures and drawings of people, and there were other drawings.

Pearl was looking at them as well. "These are your famous tarot cards, aren't they?"

"Yes, yes, my life's work, so to speak. But one is never satisfied. My pen is ever restless. But you have a story to tell, don't you? You have many I know, but you, Ben, you have one in particular. I'm very sure it is about this terrible war. Oh, my dears, gosh, my manners are terrible. What about your poor empty bellies? Let me get you something. I don't have much, some tea and tinned fish and meat perhaps. I might even have some bully beef. You will get a taste of the trenches from me, Ben. Wait let me see." She bustled out, then called from the scullery. "Get your story ready, Ben. I am anxious for it."

I felt completely disarmed. She brought in what seemed like a feast. We ate bread and tinned meat and fish and drank tea. I felt at home, and I wondered why it was me that she was targeting for my story, not Pearl, who had come so far.

Afterwards, she pinned me down. "Now, no more shilly-shallying. Tell Aunty Pixie your story. Tell it briefly, but don't leave out any important detail."

Having talked a lot, she now fell into expectant silence and sat gazing up at me from low down. Pearl sat with a grave and caring look.

I told her of Cello, his coming into the unit and the screaming casualty and the patrol and the shooting. I told of his desertion and his subsequent reappearance wearing a red cross apron. I told her of the court-martial and its unexpected conclusion. I told her of the cello and the song and the shooting and then of my cowardice and injury and my saving by Midnight and writing to Peal and my hospital treatment. I ran out of words, and it must have been dark outside despite getting close to summer.

As I hardly finished she interrupted. "Ben, tomorrow you will go to the parents of this boy again."

"I will come too," said Pearl without hesitation.

"Yes, you will both go, and you will take something with you."

"What? I don't have his cello to return to them."

"No, it will be something else. But first, you need to send a telegram to say you are coming. You can go now to the telegraph office and send it. The post office will be closed, but the Western Union office is still open. But first, tell me in a few words … what did your cello player look like?"

I gave her a description and then having received a mental map of the telegraph office, I was ushered out of the house to send the telegram.

On returning some thirty minutes later, Pixie had almost finished the first part of her work. "Oh, my boy, you have been quick. Well, we are coming on with your gift to the cello parents." She had erected a small easel and sat up right behind it, poised. Pearl sat behind her.

Pixie lifted the oblong of parchment attached to a type of board and turned it.

The light was low, but the picture seemed to have its own light and life, created by heavy black pencil on white parchment. There in front of me was Cello. His head was thrown back, but he still had his helmet on. Beside his face, which was more of an impression than a true likeness, was the ornate curl of the cello head with its fingerboard and strings extending down from Cello's left hand holding the neck of his instrument. On his face was the hint of a mischievous, almost secret yet energised laugh as he threw his music out in defiance. The right elbow was lifted, and the hint of a straight bow was scorched across the paper, as if in a flashing gesture.

"That's him!" I cried out. I just stared.

"Not quite finished yet," said Pixie. She got up and lifted a draping on a low table to reveal a gramophone. I had seen them, but my parents did not have one. She rifled through a box next to it and drew out a covered black record, a large black disc. "This is it," she said and, having carefully dusted it, put it on the gramophone. She wound the handle and then lifted the brass horn that had been folded away. "Do you recognise this?" She put the record on the turntable.

There were a few scratches at the beginning then a cello came through clearly. I listened. "Yes, I do," I said, but couldn't give any other detail.

"Bach, Number One Suite in G major. I think this was part of your story."

My mind went back. After Cello declared himself as a cellist, as I had explained to my Company Commander in the hospital, the president of the court seemed to have some difficulty understanding anything and how Cello as a classical musician should be there in front of him. Then he cleared the court angrily. We had all returned to our rooms. I was with Cello, as I had been for most of the time that he was not in court. He immediately took up his instrument. He was angry as well, but he seemed to take his anger out in his playing, attacking the cello. After he had finished, he seemed calmer. Then we heard voices and a shot. Rounds being let off were not unusual in the logistics area. If you were not involved, they were none of your business. The next day, the president who had been a colonel, was not there. I was told by one of the MPs that he had shot himself, though this would not have been the official story.

While the cello record had been playing, Pixie was at work again, this time with coloured pencils. The music as only a little over two minutes long, but without a word she put the record back on and a third time and a fourth. Pearl and I did not speak, but we did exchange glances, and I noticed that she swayed slightly to the music.

Finally, Pixie rested. The work had been so quick, so instinctive. After the music, she worked on more slowly and carefully before finally laying aside all her pencils and crayons. "Do you want to see it?"

"Of course." Pearl beat me to the reply.

Pixie again turned the board around.

"Oh it's divine," cried Pearl.

There was a sacredness about the picture that confronted us. Lashings of colour from deepest blue to bright orange flashed across a sort of deep sky behind cello. The bands of colour matched the actions of the bow of the cello in the record, backwards and forwards in a darting motion, then looping over the top of a sun rising in the corner. Well, it had been dawn when Cello was shot.

Cello himself, now coloured with a dark brown of the uniform and helmet and a pale face, stood out from the sky behind him. Yet his joy in the creation of the colours was still there in his face.

I just sort of shook my head stupidly but smiled, and I think tears came to my cheeks.

"Do you think this will be a fitting memorial for his dear parents?" asked Pixie.

"Oh yessss, very," I finally managed to stammer.

"Well, one last thing. I will frame it for you, and it will be ready for you to take first thing. You must be off at dawn, you know, so off you two sweeties go and get rest. I know how tired you must be. Come let me show you to your room. A curtain separates the bed and the couch, but you don't have to use it." She giggled.

I must have coloured up.

"Oh, come on, dears, this terrible war has brought so many together. So many loves have been found. Don't stand in the way of yours."

Suddenly, almost without thinking, a question came to me out of nowhere. "Pixie, you know a lot. What does the word *Invictus* mean.

"*Invictus*, Latin. Let me see. I might be able to ... wait a minute ... with Latin, you have to separate the word out, like English, so *victus*, I think that is, food, victuals ... no, it can't be, or *victus*, victory. No, that's 'Victoria'." She sighed in annoyance, not at me. She turned to her bookshelf and took one down. After a few moments, she looked up. "Close, but actually it's defeat, so *Invictus* means 'undefeated'."

Something dropped from or into my mind, I didn't know which. "Thank you," I said.

It was impossible to speak when Pixie was in full flow. But once inside the room and she was gone, Pearl and I looked at each other, and she smiled, putting her head slightly on one side as she had done in the aliens' shed at the dock. "She seems to have a premonition about us," I said.

"About everything."

I felt I knew what to do. "You aren't afraid of me, or anything, are you?" I said.

"No, I'm not Benjamin."

She stood there, and her waist seemed small, yet her demeanour strong. I approached her and put my hand slowly around her waist. "You are tired from your journey, and we have a difficult day ahead, so let me draw the curtain and allow you to sleep. Look, there is water and a towel for you to freshen up even."

I sat on the couch and began to take off my boots. "Thank you for agreeing to come with me tomorrow," I said towards the closed curtain.

"It will be a pleasure" came the reply.

As I lay down, I thought that it would be anything but a pleasure.

Chapter 28

A Temporary Closure
✳ ✳ ✳

I awoke to sounds of discreet knocking on the door. "Warm water for washing, my dears. I'll leave it outside." This woman was better than an aunt. She was more than a nurse.

I got up, pulled my braces up and crept outside to find a large enamel jug steaming slightly. I took it in and heard stirrings behind the curtain. "Pixie has warmed some water for us to wash."

"Oh, wonderful." She sounded sleepy.

I pushed the jug behind the curtain, without pulling it back. "Thank you, Benjamin, and good morning. I'm glad you are still here."

"Why would I not be?"

"Well everything has happened so quickly, and you weren't in my dreams, so I thought yesterday itself might have been a dream."

"Well it did seem like a dream, a good one, but I am still here, Pearl."

With a shock, I realised that this was the first time I had actually used her name, while she had used mine on several occasions.

We both appeared into the front room, where Pixie had laid out some tea and porridge. "I have made one addition to your present," she said, pulling the parchment, now in a brown frame, out of a bag she had conveniently found for it.

Along the lower half of the picture, she had engraved the words of the song "Invictus" in black pencil. It made it perfect, and I said so.

"Now you must go." She urged us on. It was barely seven o'clock.

"But has there been a reply to the telegram?" asked Pearl.

"I don't expect one. But they will be there. Where else would they go?"

In fact, as we were leaving, the telegram boy approached the house. I stopped and asked to whom it was addressed and it was me. The text was three words: **WE AWAIT YOU STOP.**

The journey was uneventful except for the many stares we received. We did not talk much. The tickets took most of my money, but I was bold now, more than I knew. Everything had changed, and I was a new man. But would Cello's parents accept me as such?

We did not have long to wait and find out. Changing trains at Waterloo shortened the journey. The one to Reading seemed to go swiftly.

We walked together up the hill towards Coley Avenue. I did manage to squeeze Pearl's hand once. "You are still not afraid, are you?"

"I am a little afraid now, yes."

"I thought so. Me too. The telegram did not indicate that we will be welcome."

Suddenly Pearl turned to me. "Did you mention that I would be accompanying you?"

I stopped dead. "No, I didn't … I … didn't think, I'm sorry."

"Well, no matter. What's done's done and what will be will be, as my nana used to say."

"Yes, we use those words too."

We dropped to silence as I tried to remember the route. We asked a passing tradesman who directed us with shocked expression and backwards glances.

We arrived and knocked at the black door inset into a porch which did not face the sun. Finally, it was eased open. Cello's father looked visibly older.

"Good afternoon, sir."

"Good afternoon, Corporal Routledge."

"May I present Mrs Pearl Johnston, who is accompanying me."

He sniffed. "What business does Mrs Johnston have with the matter, may I ask?" He did not address Pearl directly.

"Oh, she is the widow of the soldier who rescued me when I got injured, and she has supported me in my recovery and has helped procure something that we have brought you."

"I see. Well, you had better come in then."

We were shown into the front room, where we sat on our own for several minutes. Eventually, a rustling and footsteps on the wooden floor outside brought cello's mother slowly into the room, followed by the father. She went straight to Pearl. "How do you do? I gather your husband was killed. You have my condolences."

Pearl rose instantly and almost curtsied. She took the offered hand very gently. "I am grateful, madam."

"Please sit, both of you. And you, Benjamin, are you fully recovered? I must say, you are looking well."

"Yes, I am a lot better now, thank you."

"Good. Well, it would be very pleasant if we could say the same, but sadly things have not changed for us, and every day our pain is renewed."

Her husband joined in. "And we have had not a single word to give us comfort and relief … So, tell me, what news do you bring?"

"I fear I have no good news about the cello. It is my fault, as I should have secured it myself. I was content to believe that it would be returned to you with other effects. But as to the burial, I can confirm that a burial would have taken place in one of the temporary sites in the Arras area, and I know that the location will be made known to you … But I … we have come to try to present to you as best I can the story of what happened and the injustice that led to the death of your son."

"Well, you have to tell us then."

I recounted as best I could the whole story again as I had the day before to Pixie. I tried to choose my words more carefully. I did not take anything away from my guilt and my responsibility. I blamed myself for not addressing the issue at the court-martial, for not asking to take the witness stand and tell everything as I saw it. I blamed myself and said that I had been a coward whilst Cello had shown bravery in both the incident and the court-martial.

They both sat very still throughout. I paused as I ran out of breath.

"War is war. You have made amends," said Cello's father.

"We have one other thing to do which we hope might help you to come to terms with the loss, at least of the cello."

Wordlessly Pearl handed the bag to me. "This was created by a friend of Pearl's in London. Her name is Pamela Colman Smith. She is an artist and writer. She felt it might help you capture the last moments of your son … and having been there myself, I can tell you that it captures the aura of that moment when Marcus played, and we sang this song. The words are here … That moment will live with me forever."

I handed over the picture.

They looked at it in silence for what seemed like minutes. Then the mother's eye and face were suddenly glistening and wet, and she clutched the picture to herself. Her shoulders began to shake. The father moved to her and patted her a little on the shoulder.

Pearl moved closer to her and finally spoke gently. "War is madness. Now with this war, there are no limitations because everyone caught in it has become a casualty; your son, you, my husband, me and Ben. The loss takes away our control because the life we had foreseen is gone. Justice is a casualty also and a slave to the madness. Your son's death was a casualty of that madness. But he was brave in its face. Without a rifle, he was braver than the rest. One day that bravery will be recognised. "

The words held themselves in the silence of the house like the scuttling of a suddenly heard rat.

Eventually, the mother replied, "Oh one day, will it? And when will that day come?" Her face was staring out blankly. The father sat motionless. But his head was slightly bowed.

After saying goodbye we walked back to the station in the rain without talking.

We arrived back in London late and walked to the house. It was still raining. Pixie wasn't inside, so there was no respect to pay or smiles of well-being to exchange. We were able to slip into Pearl's room. Pixie had given our love her approval, which was far more powerful than a thousand disapproving looks and whispered words. Our trip to Cello's parents had given us a piece of shared history. We now had leave, and we took it avidly. Again without speech, a physical communication began in the darkness which needed nothing besides and didn't ask whether black or white or from England, Jamaica, Germany or beyond, because with the touching, so began the healing.

She even laughed a little when her leg touched my bag, a reaction for which I was to hold a lifelong gratitude.

End

About the Author

Robert J Fanshawe is an ex-British Royal Marines Officer whose uncle was killed in the First World War. With a lifelong interest in the poetry and men involved in the war, he has written three plays. *The Cellist's Friend* is the first of a trilogy of novels set in and after the war. Robert also writes non-fiction and some poetry. He lives with his family in London and is also greatly interested in sport and the performing arts.

Printed in the United States
By Bookmasters